Praise for *To Get to You*

"*To Get To You* is a story that captured my attention from page one. The tenderness of the budding relationship between Riley and Becca melted me, but it was the fragile relationship between Riley and his father that spoke to my heart."
- Stephanie Morrill, author of the Ellie Sweet series

"*To Get To You* captured my heart right from the first chapter. Riley is such a lovable character--wounded, vulnerable, but also hopeful. As for Bischof's writing, all I can say is, 'More, more, more!'" **- Melissa Tagg, author of *From the Start* and *Three Little Words***

"Another winning story from acclaimed author Joanne Bischof! Regrets, poor choices, and broken relationships are beautifully paralleled with the pure and lovely hope of renewal and new beginnings." **- Elizabeth Byler Younts, author of The Promise of Sunrise series**

"A road trip book, told from the young hero's point of view, this contemporary read shows the author's ability to create a setting and feeling that everyone can relate to. I read this book over a long weekend, and it has lingered in my thoughts ever since."
- Ashley Ludwig, author of *Mammoth Secrets*

JOANNE BISCHOF

To *get* to you

a Wild

Air

n o v e l

To Get to You
By Joanne Bischof

ISBN-13: 978-1514637500
ISBN-10: 1514637502

ALSO BY JOANNE BISCHOF

This Quiet Sky

The Cadence of Grace series:
Be Still My Soul
Though My Heart is Torn
My Hope is Found

"If it weren't for second chances we'd all be alone."

- Gregory Alan Isakov

PROLOGUE

December 24

Riley Kane propped a cut balsam tree upright and nabbed his utility knife from the back pocket of his jeans. The middle-aged couple he was assisting watched in anticipation as he slit the cords binding the Christmas tree closed. Branches bounced free in the crisp California mountain breeze. With a shake of the trunk, Riley turned and fluffed the tree to look its best as Nat King Cole sang "O Little Town of Bethlehem" *way* too slowly from the stereo in the feed store window.

Despite the fact that the tree was one of only a handful left, the wife went happy-nostalgic and the husband pulled out his wallet.

Gotta love tourists.

Riley grinned and tugged off his work gloves. He was good at choosing trees. Sure, other eighteen-year-olds had more impressive skills, but he could find the right one for a family on the first or second try. Some liked tall, others bushy. Ladies usually fingered soft branches, wanting something fragrant. This one was as close as one could get on the afternoon before Christmas. Especially ten minutes before closing.

"Would you like me to write up a sales slip?" Riley asked.

"Please." The man dug through the pockets of his snow jacket. "Do you take debit cards?"

"Just checks or cash, sorry. We don't have a machine." Riley unwound the strand of wire that secured the price tag in place, then motioned the weekenders into the feed store.

The log building held the earthy smell of feed pellets and horse treats. The couple strolled past the warm, wood-burning stove in the corner while Riley grabbed the receipt book. Thanks to a forever-broken cash register, he jotted down the price, and with a few taps on the calculator, added in the tax. The wife brought over a tin bird feeder and small bag of seed. Working Christmas Eve wasn't ideal—but he was *this* close to funding his dream snowboarding trip. He reminded himself of that as he scratched out the total and started again.

He tore off the pink slip, slid it across the antique,

wooden counter, and the husband scribbled pen to check. While tugging mittens from her puffy vest, the wife asked Riley where he was from.

That question again.

He slipped the check into the already full register. "Uh...mostly *Hawaii.*" He didn't mean to pronounce it natively, but it always came out that way. How he remembered his dad saying it.

Riley slipped the pen beside the register and straightened his beanie. While he certainly had skin more golden than this woman—along with hair and eyes that were both nearly black—it wasn't full Pacific Island blood that ran through his veins. Just a half, really. But it was enough to make people ask about the origins that he had spent most of his life trying to forget.

At least she didn't recognize him. That was always so much worse.

Finished, he pushed the drawer closed and within minutes had the tree bundled and strapped to the top of their SUV. The guy tipped him, so Riley slipped the three bucks into his back pocket while the couple climbed into their car. They drove away—green, needled branches bobbing atop the ski rack as their Durango pulled onto the icy highway.

Riley glanced to the west and eyed the sun. An hour from setting. The only place he wanted to be now was home. The shop owner, Mr. Lawrence, latched the back gate. So his sixty-year-old boss wouldn't have to do it, Riley walked across the thin layer of snow to the edge of the highway and angled the wooden *Open* sign to *Closed*.

Mr. Lawrence went about his usual motions of closing up. He brought in sacks of chicken scratch and put display bales of hay in the nearby shed.

"I can finish up. You head on home." Riley hefted one of the bales and toted it into the crowded space. He reached for a fifty-pound sack of horse feed and hoisted it to his shoulder with a grunt.

Mr. Lawrence slid a small sack into the shed. "You sure?"

"Absolutely." Riley lowered the horse feed into place. "I got this."

With a nod of gratitude, the gray-haired man disappeared inside the main shop and came out a minute later with a paper gift bag. He held it open for Riley. Inside, a loaf of some kind of bread rested beside an envelope.

He looked at his boss. "For me?"

"Merry Christmas."

Riley took the bag and thanked the man, then asked him to thank his wife for the bread.

"You got it." Mr. Lawrence tipped his cowboy hat, then lifted a weathered hand in farewell. He started down the path that led to the lower acreage of the farm. The place he and Mrs. Lawrence had spent the last thirty years of their lives.

Alone, Riley glanced at the weathered clock on the side of the feed store. With it being two minutes past closing, he went about the traditional motions of piling the leftover Christmas trees on the side of the highway. Beside three scraggly Douglas firs and one nice-looking balsam, he used a permanent marker to write *FREE* on a piece of cardboard.

That's when he heard crunching footsteps and the gentle whir of a sled over snow. Riley glanced over as a teenage girl about his own age trudged nearer. Not a common sight at this spot on the rural highway where foot traffic was next to none. The girl slowed and smiled sheepishly at him before looking at the cast-offs. Her long ponytail slipped from her shoulder as she bent to finger different branches. Riley stepped back to give her room. She turned over the smaller trees...but her eyes kept wandering to the big balsam that didn't belong in the reject heap.

"Is this one free?" she asked, peeking back at him with brown eyes so curious and gentle that he couldn't find his tongue.

He nodded dumbly.

After steering her sled to it, she began to tug the massive tree onto the wooden slats—to no gain.

And here he was standing mute like a moron when he should step in. "Let me help you with that."

She thanked him, and Riley heaved the nylon-bound beast onto her sled. Needles poked his skin now that he didn't have his gloves. Finished, he tugged off his black beanie and pushed his hair off to the side before replacing the cap. He knew people came for free trees on the evening before Christmas, but a few minutes after closing was sort of shiesty. And a sled? What was this, 1893?

Apparently, because she wore a fluttery floral skirt that looked like it had been cut from his great-aunt's couch. And between her scarf, sweater, mittens, and leggings, she had on so many layers she looked like a cross between Heidi and the sale rack at the Goodwill. Which, strangely, was kind of cute. Despite himself, he felt a smile form.

The girl looked uncomfortable by his scrutiny, then

glanced from the small studs in his ears to the skull t-shirt he shouldn't have worn to work. Without dropping his gaze, Riley zipped up his Carhartt jacket. Now it was her turn to smile.

"Thank you for the tree," she said gently.

The wind shifted and cold air pressed against his neck, his face. Stirred her hair. "Sure."

She turned to angle her sled away, and knowing that was that, Riley shifted his gaze—and his thoughts—toward home.

Time for some Top Ramen, his iPod, and the recliner in his dive of a cabin. Which reminded him—he had his tunes with him. He slid one of the earbuds into place and heard Jeff Buckley covering "Hallelujah."

Looking like she'd stepped out of a historical novel, the girl started off the way she'd come. Her shoes slipped in the slush with the weight of the tree. She pulled, then slipped again. Slowly, Riley tucked his earbuds back into his pocket.

She tugged. But her boots slipped more and she nearly fell.

Riley rubbed the back of his neck. He watched the girl struggle, knowing he could either step in and help or head on home and let her figure this out. The second idea pulled him, but the first nagged at his conscience. Judging by the fact that she had come on foot, she likely lived just up the road. She clearly wasn't getting anywhere fast, it would be dark in an hour, and he was kind of feeling like a jerk just standing there.

Heaving out a sigh, he stepped around her and eased the rope into his own hand. "Want help with that?"

Mr. Lawrence would have wanted him to. That was the motto at the Harmony Farms Christmas tree lot—to spread cheer and the kindness of the season.

Not exactly his strong suit, so he tried to ignore the way he was freezing his hind end off.

She eyed the tree as if knowing it was larger than the usual freebie. Then she glanced to the stack again. "I'll get one of the smaller ones."

Which would be awesome because then he could go home. But the other trees weren't nearly as nice. Ugh. He was going to regret this. "No need. I'm off now. I can help you."

She blinked at him with wide eyes. Not scared wide. Pretty wide. The next thing he knew, he was heading back to the store to finish closing up. He grabbed the bag Mr. Lawrence had given him, carried it out, then pulled the plug on the strands of lights. The air around the store dimmed from warm and festive to cool, quiet. Early evening shadows drew long across the snowy lot.

Everything went still. No one in sight but her and him. Acres upon acres of forest.

This was probably a bad idea.

But he locked the door and started toward the highway where she stood. He took up the rope of the sled again and tucked his bag against the tree. Within moments he was walking along with it all in tow.

Looking up curiously, she fell in step beside him. The hem of her skirt brushed the snow and his boots forged a path where they'd never gone before.

"I'm Riley," he said.

"Becca."

Right. Rebecca Fletcher. He searched her face again and suddenly remembered her from Vacation Bible School...years ago. They'd both been much smaller, and there were Dixie cups of tap water and animal crackers between them.

They walked on a few more steps, him dragging the heavy sled.

"Are you sure you don't mind?" she asked.

"Not at all." Was it bad to lie on Christmas Eve? He envisioned coal in his stocking, then remembered that there was no one to leave coal *in* his stocking.

At the shot of melancholy, he cleared his throat.

He tugged the heavy load along, wishing for his Jeep. But the XJ was in the shop with a leaking radiator and this girl probably didn't take rides from strangers. Which would make this a good time to try and set her at ease. Especially since they were nearing the part of the mountain inhabited only by foxes and squirrels.

"I haven't seen you around church lately." Hopefully the *good boy* angle would help with the awkwardness. He didn't mention that after a few years away and twice as many 'heart-to-hearts' with the police, he'd just begun attending again.

"We've been going to the Baptist church instead. It's closer and we can walk."

Which was probably code for not having a car. "Gotcha."

Overhead, the sky was clear with the coming sunset blasting pink over the mountain peaks. A car sped by, throwing up icy gravel. Was the snow getting deeper? The sled seemed to get heavier by the minute. "How far is it to your house?"

"About a mile from here." Then she said something about it being *just a trailer.*

A trailer…

He was going to have to do some fancy trimming to this tree.

"Want me to pull the sled?" she asked.

Her scuffed Doc Martens seemed small beside his black combat boots. "Uh…" He tossed his head to the side to get his stupid bangs out of his eyes. "You tried that already, remember?"

Her brows lifted. He didn't mean to blurt that out so lamely.

But she laughed softly, making brassy earrings dance against her neck.

When the sled wedged on a root sticking out of the snow, he had to stop and adjust the runners. "Do you always get your trees at Harmony Farms?" he asked once he had everything in motion again.

"Every time. A neighbor picked one up for us last year."

"On Christmas Eve?"

She nodded, pursed her lips, and looked down as a rosy hue tinted her cheeks.

Riley's brow pinched. "A guy with gray hair driving an old pickup truck?"

"That's right." Becca rubbed her hands together.

"I'm amazed you remember."

"He said it was for a family with a bunch of kids, so Mrs. Lawrence threw in a couple of poinsettias." Riley remembered loading up all of those potted plants that would have just gone to waste.

The girl beside him smiled. She had a friendly face. A nice face. A gentleness in the way she walked and kept her hands clasped in front of her skirt that showed she hadn't meant for him to do anything for her. Maybe that's why he kept glancing at her with every few steps.

Why didn't he remember her from school? He asked if she went to the one on the hill.

"No. I just graduated. A little early. But I was homeschooled."

Explained the outfit. But it was probably wiser to say, "Did you like that?"

She nodded. "It has its advantages. I got to do schoolwork in my p.j.'s and I'm always done by lunch."

"I'm a little jealous." He chuckled.

Leaving the edge of the highway, he followed her into the woods. A direction that was probably a shortcut. Snow fell so softly that he hadn't noticed it before. They were both quiet. Feeling the aloneness of their surroundings, he tried to think of something to say to make her comfortable. She had lit up about that poinsettia deal, so he asked more about her family. She talked easily for a while, and by the time they dipped into the valley where small cabins and trailers speckled the snowy woods, he learned that she had five brothers and sisters, her father was a truck driver for a local dairy, and though he was gone a lot, was the best dad in the world.

Riley wasn't about to argue. He didn't have a dad. At least not one that counted. Dipping his head, he watched the ground and tried to shove off any thoughts of where the man might be or what he was doing. If he even cared that it was Christmas or that he had a son.

"What about you?" Becca asked.

"Uh...my mom and I lived here for a while after my dad left. We moved around a lot since then, mostly in Orange County, but I came back here after I graduated. She's a cheerleading coach back at one of the high schools."

For the last few years there were girls in little skirts every time he turned around. Which had been its own kind of complication.

Becca was still looking at him thoughtfully. Clasping her mittened hands again, she asked about his dad.

He shouldn't have talked about himself at all. "Um...

he's a surfer."

Her eyebrows lifted.

"I know, that doesn't seem like a real occupation, but he gets paid for it...has sponsors...travels the world. He lives in Hawaii, which is where he's from. I get postcards from time to time." Which went straight into the trash because that's all there ever was.

Hot from pulling the tree along, Riley unzipped his jacket and tossed it onto the loaded sled. He left his beanie on to cover his psycho hair that was more mop top than mohawk lately. He'd attacked it with electric clippers a few weeks ago—sort of his therapy on bad days—and he really didn't want to advertise that to this girl just now.

But she wasn't looking at his beanie. Or his hair.

She was looking at his eyes, and there was something in her gaze that had him wondering just how much she saw. How much had he said?

He needed to look somewhere else, so Riley tilted his head up, letting his gaze rise all the way up the tops of the pines towering above. Remembering the way he used to build Lego fortresses with their own kinds of turrets and towers, imagining that he could keep the world at bay.

He'd build drawbridges just so he could lower and lift them. Pretending that such a place could actually exist for him. A place where people couldn't get in—not unless he wanted them to. A wish that the plastic chains could be real and a single command could shut out everything. In a way, he eventually succeeded. For far too many years he succeeded. But the only problem with shutting the world out was that it also shut in the pain.

With this girl looking at him as if she knew something about him that he hadn't said, Riley wished for a real-life drawbridge to raise up. So she wouldn't *see*. But when she started walking again and asked if he'd worked at the feed store long, the change in subject was so abrupt, so tenderly worded and considerate, that he knew it was too late.

Snow dusted the top of her light brown hair.

The sweet sight of it made it hard for him to pull his gaze away. But if he didn't watch where he was going, he'd smack into a tree. Glancing up, he saw a weathered, silver Airstream trailer in the distance.

"A couple of years," he answered weakly. With the money he made at the feed store *slash* Christmas tree lot, he covered his rent and lived like a king on microwavable meals and Snickers bars. He left that last part out and just looked at the trailer with its wreath hanging from the narrow, metal door.

The end of the road, then.

She turned to him. "Thanks for the help. I'm sure you want to get back." She said the last sentence slowly—as if she didn't want to.

Riley heaved the heavy sled to a standstill and found the words just coming out. "I can set the tree up…uh…if you want. I do lots of deliveries, so tree installation is kind of a specialty of mine."

"*Tree installation*?"

"It's a real thing." He was such an idiot.

Her eyes were bright and he realized she was humoring him. "Come on in then." Next, she offered him a smile and a cup of cider. "It's just the powdered kind. But my sisters and I made sugar cookies today."

"I like both of those." And despite how he was feeling earlier, he kind of wanted to be around to witness her siblings' reaction to this larger-than-life tree. He didn't have brothers and sisters. His family just consisted of him and his mom, and right now…

Just him.

If he were honest with himself, he wanted to spend a few more minutes with this girl. Even if it was only the half hour it would take to get the tree set up. He wasn't sure what to make of that. With a light in her eyes, she motioned toward the trailer.

His mouth quirked as he hoisted the tree and followed her up the steps. "I'm going to have to trim at least a foot off the bottom of this thing," he said.

"Can we—"

"Show it to them first?"

She scrunched her nose with clear delight.

Becca opened the door. A tingle hit his cheeks at the shrieks that filled the air when he lugged the tree inside. Beaming faces and kids of all sizes rushed him. He could barely make out Becca's own smiling face as he hefted the fragrant balsam into the small space. Riley freed his utility knife. After a few slices, the bindings fell to the ground and green branches burst free.

The trailer all but shook with excitement. Shouts and whoops sounded all around. Becca hoisted a toddler onto her hip, looked at him with shining eyes, and from a nearby stereo, Nat King Cole sang "O Little Town of Bethlehem"…kind of perfectly.

ONE

Three weeks later

Earbuds tucked into place, Riley slipped his iPod into the pocket of his hoodie and trudged down the frozen edge of the highway. His black combat boots crunched the gravel lining the mountain road. Through his headphones, Lord Huron was playing "She Lit a Fire" as a minivan whizzed by, blasting him with icy air. Riley would have driven his Jeep the two plus miles to the Fletchers', but it was still in the shop. And he really needed to see Becca.

He shoved his hair out of his eyes only to have to do it again a few seconds later. Cold air prickling his skin, he pulled up the hood of his black sweatshirt, then rubbed his palm across the snowboard emblem. As the road crested the summit, he did too.

He tugged his cell phone out of the back pocket of his jeans and eyed the screen that had been black all day. Leave it to him to lose his charger. Since it was his Friday off, he and Becca had planned for an evening walk with her family, and since he couldn't remember what time he was supposed to be at her place, he figured erring on the side of caution was best.

Riley pocketed his cell. Even if his phone was working, the text would go to her mom first. Which, surprisingly, he was getting used to, because before he could even ask Becca for her number on Christmas Eve, she'd confessed to not having her own phone.

Instead, she'd jotted down her mom's cell number for him. Then she'd hurried to add that he could write her a letter if he'd rather do that. He'd taken the scrap of paper, trying to envision himself writing a letter. That night, before he could even figure out how to text a girl via a mom, his phone had beeped and it was Becca, inviting him over for Christmas day. Homeschool girls were super friendly. And apparently a little bored.

If you don't have any plans, she'd added.

Nope. No plans. Having spent the weekend before with his mom, Riley had hiked back to the Fletchers' on Christmas morning and it was one of the best days he'd ever had. Wanting to bring something, he'd grabbed two dozen doughnuts from the bakery. Not the most festive of desserts, but Mrs. Fletcher thanked him heartily and her six children did some serious damage to the contents of that box.

On that same walk now, Riley remembered how Becca's mom had even put something under the tree for him. A ten-dollar gift card for song downloads since Becca had told her that he liked music. How did they...?

His thank you felt so insufficient.

He smiled at the memory, then chewed his lip because this magic couldn't last. Fog filtered across the highway and Riley crammed his hands in his pockets. Once the Fletchers learned what he was really like, Becca might not be able to hang out with him anymore. Not that he had a death wish, but he'd gently mentioned a few reasons why over the last few weeks.

Like how while he was proud to be smoke free for almost a year now, it was probably also best to confess to her how young he had started.

Or that when he was sixteen—mixed with having a *really* bad day—he'd off and gotten his tongue pierced. He didn't have it in now and hadn't had anything in when he'd met her, but it felt wrong not to make sure she knew just what she was signing up for with him. Not like she was signing up for anything. They were really just friends. Because Becca was kind. And good.

Quaint. That was it. She reminded him of those little Swedish dolls people collected. She dressed in so many layers, he hadn't seen so much as an ounce of skin.

His last girlfriend was more like Beach Barbie.

And there he was...doing it again. *She's not your girlfriend, Riley.*

He even had proof. While saying goodbye outside her trailer on Christmas Eve, he'd been thinking of nine different ways to ask her out when he finally got the nerve to see if maybe they could get some coffee "sometime or something." Yeah, he'd said it lame like that.

She had looked a little wistful and said that she wasn't allowed to *technically* date. She'd used air quotes and explained that her parents' rule was that a guy could hang out with her and her family in a group setting, but that was it.

Hands down the first time a girl had said that to him.

His old ways would have had him walking off, but there was something about Rebecca Fletcher that had him saying, "Okay," then coming back the next day to play Monopoly with her and her third-grade brother. The day after that, he'd stood in Becca's tiny kitchen spreading peanut butter on bagels while her six-year-old sister asked why he had a skull on his t-shirt and if he liked raisins.

Yesterday, Riley had read *The Little Engine That Could* to the three-year-old twins. Did the voices and everything. He and Becca capped off the evening with a card game of Speed on the trailer floor, at which time she declared him a cheater. After losing fair and square for the fourth time, she was so cute as she threw her cards at him that he'd wanted to kiss her.

But her mom was watching them over busy knitting needles and one of the ankle-biters toddled by, spilling a cup of milk down the back of Riley's shirt, breaking him from his trance. He was starting to get used to the whole *group setting* thing.

Two motorcycles growled past, and Riley focused on the edge of the highway. He practically had to duck away from the spray of gravel from an eighteen-wheeler. Glad it was time to veer into the woods, he left the roadside for quieter ground. He trudged on, five minutes turning into ten before he slowed and hit pause on his music.

Staring at the clearing where Becca lived, Riley halted altogether.

There was no trailer.

No home. No Fletchers. He glanced around.

A few neighboring rigs sat spread about, but nothing was in the Fletchers' spot other than tire tracks in the snow and two black trash bags.

Riley turned in a quick circle. Stared at the empty spot again. He called her name. A horrible sickness rising inside him, Riley started that way. This was definitely the spot where her trailer had sat. He remembered the faded yellow mobile home with blue Christmas lights next to it. But there was no Becca.

Music blasted in his ears when his thumb bumped the play button on his iPod. The volume bar must have slid up in his pocket because now he was going to be deaf. Riley yanked the screeching earbud free, then rubbed his ear at the lingering ache. He turned in another circle, slower this time, and remembered his dead cell in his pocket. He tugged it out and hit the power button. A cold black screen taunted him. If she'd texted him, he wouldn't have even gotten it.

His heart sank lower when he spotted the Christmas tree laying behind the black trash bags. The one her posse of siblings had decorated once he finally got the lights strung. A Christmas record had turned and crackled from a player as Becca—who apparently knew every word to every Christmas song—sang "Baby, It's Cold Outside" like no one was in the room.

A sick emptiness hit him.

Riley walked over to the tree and with a burn in his throat, touched needles that were now brittle. A plastic grocery bag hung from one of the branches. His name was scribbled in black marker. He yanked the plastic loose and after struggling with the knot, tore inside the wrinkled bag to find a folded piece of paper. He flipped it open.

Riley – My dad's been in an accident. His semi was run off the road in New Mexico and it flipped. Witnesses said a car swerved to avoid a deer and he swerved to keep from hitting the car full of kids. They airlifted him to a hospital there. They told my mom that he's in a coma and she's freaking out and I am too. The truck's totaled and I'm really scared for my dad. He's going in for surgery. Mom's already arranged for a way to pull our trailer there so we're leaving within the hour - I think. I've tried calling you and texting. Please find this –B

Riley skidded his palm across his forehead. Not her dad. Her dad was everything to her.

He folded the paper and slipped it in his pocket, then turned to try to make sense of what he needed to do. He needed to get home. Charge his phone. He needed to see if she was all right. At a clatter from behind, Riley looked back and saw someone step out of the yellow mobile with the blue lights.

Riley rushed over. "Did you see the Fletchers leave? The family who lived just over there?" He pointed to where the time-worn Airstream had sat.

"Well…" the man said in a slow drawl, "I do believe that they headed off the hill. Not sure why." He scratched the top of his head, the tiny sound grating Riley's last nerves as the seconds wore on. "I suppose, I can't rightly tell you where they went off to. But I did see someone come and hook a big van up to the trailer, and the next thing I knew…they were gone. Like a bunch'a Gypsies."

At a loss for words, Riley made a fist and pressed it to his forehead. "Okay. Thanks."

After one last quick survey, he started back the way he'd come. Even though he was going uphill now, his steps were quicker. He was sweating by the time he got to his cabin. Riley threw his hoodie onto the drum set in the corner and hitched the door closed with his shoe.

It took forty-five minutes to find his lost cell charger, and when he did, it was only because he'd crawled under his tiny kitchen table and dumped out a shoebox of receipts, pay stubs, and gum wrappers. Riley nabbed the white cord, then rammed it into the wall. He waited the few minutes it took for his cell to begin breathing again. He crawled out from under the table and shoved the chair back so he could sit on the floor beside the outlet.

With the phone still plugged in, he powered it up. Six missed calls and four texts. Two of the calls were from Becca, but he sped through her texts first.

Are you there?

And another. *Riley. Call me.*

His heart sank as they went on. Becca trying to find him, finishing with the final text.

My dad's in the hospital and we have to go. PLEASE call me.

Riley growled and tapped the code for his voicemail. She didn't sound frantic as he would have thought. She was calm, but one of the twins was crying in the background and Becca hummed gently, surely to comfort the little kid. Then the whir of a diesel engine drowned out her voice even as she seemed to explain that the Baptist church had lent them the youth group van. She finished with a goodbye, and never had Riley's fingers moved so fast as he punched the contact for her mom and waited as it rang on the other end.

No one answered.

He left as polite a message as he could form, telling Mrs. Fletcher that he was so sorry about the accident, said that his phone had died but that he finally got Becca's messages. And for either of them to call him if they needed anything. He hung up feeling empty.

Still sitting on the floor next to the outlet, he didn't move for a few minutes. The last words he and Becca had shared face to face, he'd confessed the hardest thing he would ever have to say to her and it had nearly left her in tears. And now he couldn't fix it.

He couldn't fix anything for her.

His stomach grumbled and he ignored it. A few minutes later it did it again, so he rose, just wanting to go to bed. He grabbed a banana and a granola bar, downing both with a glass of water from the tap. He moved the cell-charging operation to his nightstand, and since it was only six, sat looking blankly at a Jeep magazine until he got tired enough to sleep.

Rising, Riley shed his jeans and shirt for some sweat pants. Then he crawled under the gray comforter. He tried to sleep but just missed Becca, so he found his gift card and downloaded a new song—finally drifting off to the 1949 recording of Margaret Whiting and Johnny Mercer's "Baby, It's Cold Outside."

TWO

"How did you get so good on a board?"

The question Becca had asked as they sat at the skate park in town.

CJ was on a scooter while Tyler—on rollerblades—stared wide-eyed at the ledge Riley had just kicked a three-sixty off of.

"I dunno." Skateboard still under his shoes, Riley pulled off his helmet.

"Now I see why you got those offers from sponsors." Sitting beside him in jeans and the Converse he got her as a late Christmas present, she'd smiled, eyebrows raised in question.

Riley had dipped his head. What to say to that? He didn't want that life. For so many reasons. *"I think I'll stick with the feed store."* He flexed an arm. *"I'm pretty good at lifting hay bales."*

Grinning, she pushed against his chest.

He took that moment to change the subject. *"How about we talk about you instead, little fashion designer."*

She smirked. The night before, she'd showed him her sketchbook filled with designs. Soft angles and girly cuts—the kinds of things she wore. Bohemian, she'd called it. Beyond proud of her, he hinted that she should add some guy stuff. *"I'll totally rock your line."*

Becca had laughed.

At a buzzing near his ear, Riley sat up with a jolt and smacked his head on the window frame. His cell phone buzzed again so loud it nearly vibrated right off the nightstand. The daydream falling away, Riley slapped his hand over the phone and ran his wrist over his eyes to try and read the caller ID.

Mrs. Fletcher.

He slammed his thumb on the green button. "Hello?"

"Riley?"

At the sound of the voice on the line, his heart shot up. "Becca!"

"Oh my gosh, it's you."

"I tried calling you. I'm so sorry about your dad."

In the span of a few breaths, Becca shared that her dad was still in a coma and that the ER nurse told her mom that they'd inserted a breathing tube and had to do some other stuff. He had a few broken ribs and what was likely a concussion. A broken wrist and leg.

Riley rubbed his eyes with his palm. "Are you serious?" he asked softly.

"I want to see him so bad. We're in Arizona still. Maybe another day away. It's slow going with the trailer and all the kids. We keep having to stop and the gas is insane—" She clipped that last word off quickly as if regretting having said that.

"Is there anything…anything I can do?"

"No, I don't think so. I'm sorry I blurted that out. Mom has enough for gas and all that and we don't have to pay for hotels because we've brought our house with us."

The words were so light, he wondered how much she'd been trying to be cheerful for others over the last twenty-four hours. "Becca."

"Yeah."

"It's going to be okay."

She went totally quiet which meant she was trying not to cry.

He leaned forward. If there was some way he could help… "Who's driving that big van?"

"My mom. It's a beast and she's never driven a car this big. She's seriously going to kill us all." There was a genuine spark of humor to her voice and Riley smiled.

"Are you sure there's nothing I could do? Can I come..." He couldn't believe these words were about to pop out. "...come help you guys somehow?"

She went quiet again for a second. "You'd do that?"

"Yeah." He would.

Her voice was soft. "What about your job and everything?"

"Becca, I work at a feed store selling hay and squirrel food in a town that only has one stop sign. That's hardly a happening business." He sat up farther, the idea coming together. "I think Mr. Lawrence could cover for a week or two, easy. I need to get my Jeep fixed, which shouldn't take too long."

He had some savings set aside to go snowboarding in Utah this year, but he could go to the auto shop today and have the radiator replaced by nightfall instead. It was in line behind some SUV, but he could expedite the process. Especially if he brought Chuck, the mechanic, a California burrito and threatened to tell the local newspaper just who was responsible for the tree-lighting ceremony catastrophe. Jeep? Fixed.

Then the rest of the savings would be gas and he'd be set.

"I'd have to talk to my mom," she said, hope in her voice.

"Please do."

"That would be amazing if you were here. I don't really know how to describe it, but it just would be."

He smiled at that. "I could help your mom with the van and if you need extra hands with the kids while she's with your dad—whatever. I'll do whatever you need."

"I think she'd be so grateful for that. But are you sure it wouldn't be too much trouble? It's such a long way."

"Let's pretend like I need a vacation."

He heard a smile in her words. "Hanging out with the Fletcher clan at a hospital is not exactly a vacation."

"Hmm...maybe I *should* run that one by my travel agent."

She laughed.

"Seriously. I want to help you." He wanted to be useful. And he hated the idea of Becca and her mom trying to balance so much...or any one of those kids being scared as their dad fought for his life. "Talk to your mom and call me back."

"OK, I will," she said breathlessly, and after a goodbye, was gone.

Riley put his phone back on its charger and headed

for the bathroom. He showered then searched the floor of his room for something clean to wear. That was useless, so he dug in the bottom of his closet. Dressed, he ran a quick load of laundry then shoved two Pop-Tarts into the toaster only to discover that it was broken. *Super*.

Leaning back against the edge of the counter, he ate one of the pastries cold. Riley glanced to the fridge, spotting the lift schedule for his favorite resort in Utah. He downed a few more bites, trying not to think about how much he had wanted the boarding trip. How much he and one of his friends had been saving for it.

Riley's dad had taught him to snowboard when he was six. While he wobbled his way down the beginner course, his dad had captured it on his camcorder, laughing and waving the whole time. The guy had promised to teach him to surf next. The stud's real passion. But two weeks later, he told Riley that he had to go.

Just…go.

No better reason than that.

Nearly a dozen years later, Riley had no idea what his dad's voice sounded like or if he shaved every day. But the world-famous surfer probably had too many trophies to store, countless exotic stamps in his passport, and some ritzy girlfriend from one of the islands. Riley hoped there was an earthquake and his dad got knocked out by his latest first place cup.

The last time he'd heard from his dad had been on his sixteenth birthday when his mom handed him a card with a hundred-dollar bill inside. It read, *"How ya doing, kid?"* right above Jake Kane's prized signature. Riley tossed the card in the trash then used the hundred bucks to get his tongue pierced and hustle a pack of cigarettes. He spent the last twenty on an Audioslave CD, then listened to "Like a Stone" on repeat while he practiced blowing smoke rings in the Jeep that he and his mom had scrimped and saved for. Then silently thanked his dad for another awesome birthday.

Now that he was eighteen and no child support was required, Riley had moved out to make things easier on his mom. That's what he told her at least. But really, he hated Orange County because it was too close to the ocean. So he moved to this mountain town that wasn't even on the map just to get away from the sound of the waves.

The toaster whirred to life, snapping Riley from his trance. Slightly creeped out by the mood swings of his toaster, he put the second Pop-Tart in and watched the coils heat up. Now it was time to call his boss and make sure that he could get a few weeks off. Mr. Lawrence answered on the first ring—as usual—and Riley relayed the situation, followed by a request for a week or two off. Mr. Lawrence told him to make it two since the store was dead as a doornail around New Year's anyway.

Riley thanked him. Warm breakfast in hand, he crammed dirty dishes into the sink, shot out a squeeze of liquid soap, and ran hot water over everything full blast. They each said goodbye just as the washing machine chugged into action. Sliding to a halt in front of the machine, Riley poured in powdered soap. Foam rose to an awkward level. Maybe measuring would have been a good idea. He slammed the lid then went back a minute later and put a heavy box on it for good measure.

He was just finishing with the last of the dishes when his phone rang again. Riley answered it. "Becca?"

Her mom's voice spoke. "Riley, this is Pam."

Crud. He was in trouble. He stuttered out a hello.

But she didn't sound mad as she relayed what Becca had told her about him offering to come. "Is that true?"

He could practically see her expression as she asked that. Freckled face pinched in curiosity. "Yes…ma'am."

"And your job?"

"It's okay for me to take a few weeks off." He tried

not to think about his boarding trip.

Mrs. Fletcher was quiet for several moments. "And…Becca?"

Suddenly Riley wondered how much of their last face-to-face conversation had been overheard. The one where Becca had confessed to never having a guy as a friend before. Not a *close* friend. Overwhelmed by her innocence, the fact that he was the guy to get to fill the role, and the sudden rock in his gut, Riley had gently explained that he'd had girlfriends among those cheerleaders that used to hang out at his house.

And that each at their own time, they'd been a lot more than friends. Like *way* more.

He and Becca had been sitting on the trailer's sofa, the spot that would fold out to be her bed when he left. Her mom had been at the dinette doing a crossword puzzle. He'd spoken very softly because the conversation had to happen and privacy wasn't even something he was about to ask for. But his honesty had done something to Becca that scared him. There was a breaking in those eyes—that heart.

Now Riley sat on one of his dining chairs and stared at the floor. "I want to help her. And you. Your family." Was he saying the wrong thing? "I promise I'll stick to the rules you guys have set down. I know they're important to you and they are for me too." He could only hope that he'd been proving as much. "If you'll let me, I'd like to help." Mrs. Fletcher's silence broke into a thank you so splintered and so sincere, it tightened his chest. "We are so grateful for you, Riley. All of us."

She told him that she had some things stored at a friend's house in Idyllwild, about ten minutes away from where they lived in Mountain Center. She rattled off a list of items she could use to make the kids more comfortable. Riley hurried to grab a piece of paper and pencil to write things down, including a generator and two twenty-gallon water barrels since the Fletchers might not have hook-ups if they stayed in a parking lot.

"The generator is really heavy. Becca and I have to lift it together and even then it's a monster," Mrs. Fletcher said.

"I'll be all right."

She talked on and he nodded as he scribbled. His phone buzzed and Riley eyed the screen only to see a number he didn't recognize. But the area code was the same one he'd had as a kid when his dad was still around. It had to be from one of the beach cities.

And wait...he'd gotten a call from this place a week

ago.

Mrs. Fletcher was telling him something important, so Riley ignored the call and simply made sure he had the hospital address correct. Then he promised to fetch the stuff and bring it all with him to Taos, New Mexico. He might have to take the backseat out of his Jeep, but just folding it down should get it all to fit.

"I have a few five-gallon fuel jugs I can fill up for the generator when I get closer."

Never had he heard such relief in someone's voice. "Thank you, Riley. You're a godsend." The phone muffled and he heard the clang of shoes on metal steps as if she was walking in or out of the trailer. "I've found Becca and she's reaching for the phone so I'm going to pass it o—"

All he heard was Mrs. Fletcher's laughter and then there was a little phone thief in his ear. Riley grinned.

"Okay," Becca said. "This thing is dying but I just have to say drive safe, pleeeaasse." She paused, her voice getting softer. "I can't *wait* to see you."

Closing his eyes, Riley drew in a slow breath. "I'll see you in a few days." His sweetest friend. The sound of a smile lit up her words. "See you in a few days."

THREE

After the mechanic promised the Jeep would take two more hours *max*, Riley pocketed his phone and started another load of laundry. He already had an open duffle bag on his bed, and after adding socks, he crammed in a handful of t-shirts. In went hoodies and jeans. Maybe he should grab something nicer. Especially since the Fletchers probably attended a church, regardless of what state they were in. If he was going to join them, he'd need something better than faded band t-shirts. Before he could change his mind, he stashed a collared shirt in with the rest of his stuff.

It was one of the few he had, because going to church hadn't really been on his radar when he moved back here. But it was part of the deal between him, his mom, and his old counselor from Orange County. When Riley had announced that he was moving out of O.C., his counselor had put in a phone call, and before Riley could even empty his first cardboard box in this little cabin, a guy in slacks was knocking on his door. Pastor Keith. A man in glasses, bearing a loaf of banana bread that his wife had baked.

Now they met every other week for a "checkup," as they'd dubbed it. Either at the local coffee shop or just in Riley's living room, they'd sit and Keith asked about Riley's life and how things were going. Riley always shot for honesty and, as strange as it was, found that he enjoyed the accountability. Along with a narrow miss with juvie two years ago, it was another reason he worked to keep his life on track.

The washing machine thudded as it hit the spin cycle. Was he missing anything else? He'd go by the store on his way out of town to get food for the road—granola bars and stuff. If he was smart enough to remember, a case of bottled water.

Mr. Lawrence had offered to drive him the ten minutes up to Idyllwild where the Jeep was being worked on, so Riley glanced out the window even though he knew his boss wouldn't come by until noon.

Hand to the back of his head, Riley paused a moment. What was he forgetting?

One…no *two* things.

He tromped down to his bedroom and searched the mess on top of his dresser for the first—his EpiPen. He was supposed to always have one on him but usually just kept one stashed in his backpack. It had been a couple of years since he'd had an allergic reaction, but he wasn't supposed to go anywhere without it.

And now the second. Phone handy, he started a quick email to his buddy who was the other half of that boarding trip. Riley pocketed the EpiPen so he could type with two thumbs.

Hey, Ramsey. I'm going to have to miss out on the Utah trip. Sorry, man. :/ I need to help the Fletchers out with some stuff.

He and Ramsey had been friends since Riley's first day as a terrified freshman on the high school wrestling team. Two years older and ten times as mature, Ramsey had watched as Riley nearly flushed life down the drain, then stood there and picked him up when Riley realized a second chance was his for the taking. Riley had already filled his friend in on how his Christmas had gone, so the college sophomore knew all about Becca.

Riley added a few lines about what had happened to her dad. *I'll be back in a couple of weeks, tops. But the drive is going to eat up my savings.* He added another apology, regretted doing this to one of his best friends, and hit send.

Down the hallway, Riley slipped two fingers into his back pocket to make sure he had the address for the couple storing the Fletchers' generator. Standing there in the middle of his tiny cabin, EpiPen in hand, he was sure he was still forgetting something. Whatever it was…that's why they'd invented drug stores. Which reminded him—toothbrush.

He added mouthwash and gum, because minty freshness was his mantra when it came to girls. Riley shifted his mouth to the side before he forgot that he was nowhere near to kissing the lovely Rebecca Fletcher. Especially now.

Cell on the counter, he tapped it and looked at her picture on the screen—a shot of her seated on a boulder during one of their hikes through the woods. Taking in the sight of her smile, those bright eyes, he thought about how much he aimed to protect her innocence in the way that her family expected him to. And in the way that he expected of himself. Maybe two years ago his only focus would have been making it to home base, but he'd been down that road before and now he was trying to think a little more wisely. Riley glimpsed his reflection in the mirror. His very existence living proof that there was one accident too many in this world. And he didn't want to be his dad.

Pausing, Riley pinched the bridge of his nose because his reasons should have had a heck of a lot to do with God, but to his shame, that was suddenly an afterthought. Not wanting to think about any of this anymore, he scrolled through his phone contacts to be certain Pastor Keith was on speed dial, then stashed a few final things in his duffle—including a notepad and pen. He needed to tell Becca something and knew of no other way.

The rest of the morning passed in a flash as he tried to leave his cabin in somewhat decent shape. It was winter, so he shut his water off in case the pipes froze while he was gone. By the time he had moved his duffle bag and a backpack onto his tiny front porch, he saw Mr. Lawrence pulling out of the feed store driveway in the distance. One of the perks of living in a town that was about 1/8 of a mile long—he had a front row seat to all the big happenings. Folks said that if you blinked, you'd miss Mountain Center completely. Riley used to try it as a kid and it was pretty much true.

His phone buzzed and it was Ramsey.

No problem, man. Totally get it. Let me know if you need anything. Make sure you have the map right side up and don't do anything I wouldn't do.

Riley chuckled. *Will do. Thanks.* He owed him one.

A minute later Mr. Lawrence pulled his farm truck into the drive where six little cabins sat, one of which Riley rented. He heaved his bag over the tailgate with a thunk. "Thanks for giving me a ride up."

Dressed in his usual flannel shirt, Mr. Lawrence rolled down his window the rest of the way. "My pleasure."

"I owe you big time."

"You can repay me by setting up a new birdwatcher display when you get back."

Was that a dash of dry humor coming from his normally matter-of-fact boss? Riley shot a smile at the man and climbed in. "It's a deal."

The old Chevy pulled out of the dirt driveway then wound up the mountain highway. Having driven this stretch of road whenever he needed a gallon of milk or a movie to rent, Riley knew the curves by heart. Ten minutes later, the truck was chugging past quaint shops designed with tourists in mind. Couples dressed in scarves and furry boots walked the sidewalks arm in arm.

Southern Californians who had vacated the sixty-five-degree suburbs to see what a *real* winter looked like.

The truck slowed in front of the only auto shop in town. Thanking his boss again, Riley hopped out then grabbed his stuff. He patted the tailgate, and with a wave out his window, Mr. Lawrence pulled away.

Inside, the shop smelled like oil, and a shrill grinding noise made it impossible to call out for Chuck. Riley spotted the stout mechanic wedged under the passenger side of a minivan. When the grinding stopped, Riley crouched and spoke to keep from startling the guy.

"Hi."

"Hey." Grunting, Chuck gripped the edge of a back tire and wheeled his creeper out from under the car. "I have good news and bad news."

Great.

The forty-something-year-old rose to a stand then wiped greasy hands on a red rag. "The good news is that the job's only gonna cost you $180."

"That is good." Riley fished out his wallet where he'd stashed a chunk of that savings.

"The bad news is that while you have a new radiator, the transmission feels like its slipping. It probably needs to be overhauled, and I think the transfer case should be replaced as well." He held up his grubby hands peaceably. "Now…you can leave it with me for a few more days and I can see what I can do, but it'll cost somewhere between one and two grand."

All the money he *didn't* have.

"It'd be smart to do the work, but it's also not fully gone yet. I don't see why it couldn't go for a little while longer. Really, it's up to you."

Riley shifted his mouth to the side. This wasn't happening. "If I hit the road?"

The mechanic lifted dark eyebrows. "Time'll tell."

Scrubbing the back of his hair, Riley groaned.

Chuck glanced from the duffle bag and back. "Think on it for a minute. In the meantime, we can go over your invoice."

In the back office, Chuck tapped out the total on an old dusty computer.

Riley paid and signed on the dotted line. "You know? I think I'll just give it a whirl and hope for the best." He was talking a lot braver than he actually was. But hey, a slipping transmission could go for a hundred miles…or five thousand. He was going to arm wrestle with five thousand and pray he won.

"You got it." Chuck tore off a yellow receipt,

stashing the pink copy. "She's all yours." He flung the Jeep keys toward Riley who caught them before they hit the soda machine.

"Thanks."

The mechanic trailed him out to the little front parking lot. "Heading to the slopes finally?"

"I was going to." Riley reached the black Jeep and patted the roof. He hitched open the old door of the '88 and looked back at his buddy. "But there's been a change of plans."

Temper Trap – Sweet Disposition

Eagles – Take it Easy

Band of Horses – The Funeral

Lynyrd Skynyrd – Sweet Home Alabama

Riley scrolled through his latest playlist and tapped his favorite Eagles song. Smooth harmonies and a rhythm guitar filled his Jeep with the sound of the '70s as he threw it into gear. Winter air blew cold through his rolled-down window, but he propped his elbow up on the door frame and pulled out of the driveway. The curving highway led him higher toward the house where Mrs. Fletcher was storing her stuff. About a mile up the winding road, a gray fog blew across the two lanes. A minute later, tiny raindrops splattered his windshield.

Riley rolled up his window and flicked on the heater of his Jeep that was more his baby than anything else he owned. Next he fished the list from the pocket of his jeans. He skimmed the address Mrs. Fletcher had given him. After a few minutes and two U-turns, Riley finally found the old cabin set back off the beaten road, as most houses around here were. Out of his truck and up the pine needle-lined walkway, Riley knocked on the stout door of the most gingerbread-y house he'd ever seen. As he waited beneath the frilly trim, he read the combination that Mrs. Fletcher had given him in case no one was home.

A quick glance along the garage door brought him to the combination lock and he spun the code in. Becca's mom had given him clear instructions where he should be able to find her things inside the storage area, so he didn't have to hunt too long.

But holy smokes that generator was heavy.

Pretty sure he was going to regret lifting that on his own, Riley added the water jugs to the back of his Jeep.

He tossed in a few more of the necessities on Mrs. Fletcher's list including a gray and orange quilt for CJ, Becca's twelve-year-old brother. Then a bag of stuffed animals for six-year-old Anna.

Riley slammed the hatch, then glanced back, spotting a big tote labeled *Becca's fabric*. It was written in her pretty writing. He popped the top and looked inside to different colored threads and all kinds of scraps and cuttings from clothes she got at the thrift store. She had told him that she liked vintage fabric, but Riley had a hunch that it was because she couldn't afford to buy it new. A burn in his chest, he closed the lid. Then ran his fingers over the curves of her name.

Back in his truck, he pulled out his cell to call his mom. The three rings went straight to her voicemail so he left all the details of where he was headed in a message. He slipped the key in the ignition, started the engine, and steered his XJ back onto the highway. The rain picked up speed, becoming slush that meant snow for the higher elevations. Good thing he was headed downhill. Still, he cranked the heater to full blast.

Now it was just him and the open road. Fourteen hours to Taos, New Mexico.

Riley smiled.

He took Highway 74 off the mountain and hit Palm Desert by the time the rain had stopped. From there, he steered his Jeep onto the I-10 that would lead him out of the great state of California. According to his GPS, he would be on this baby for nearly 700 miles. At least he didn't have to worry about getting lost.

He shifted in the seat and tapped the blinker to veer into the fast lane. While great at off-roading, his Jeep wasn't entirely designed for speed. Still, it could hit sixty with the best of them, so he'd see Becca in two days tops.

Because she was committed to taking a relationship ultra-slow, they weren't quite to the hugging stage, which was another first for him. But that was just fine. He'd shake her hand with gusto if he had to.

A sports car came out of nowhere and zipped in front of him. Riley thumped the brakes and down-shifted just enough to miss hitting the jerk's bumper. Riley pinned his fist at his side to keep from giving the guy a piece of his mind.

As it was, the silver-haired lady driving the Volvo in the next lane was giving the hot shot a stern talking to. Likely she'd been cut off as well. She was hauling a car full of grannies who all wore red hats with purple feathery scarves. But instead of making a fuss at the driver, all the passengers were jabbering in Riley's direction. Pointing and using hand motions that he didn't understand. One of them was trying to roll down her window and seemed to be calling out if he was all right.

Confused, Riley did a double take. His Jeep made a crazy sound.

Not good. And now he was going too slow for the fast lane. He pushed the clutch and shifted forward into fifth. The gear ground and his gas pedal went limp. Sank all the way to the floorboard and stuck that way. With no gas, the car whirred and slowed. Riley shook the stick and pumped the gas as a horn blared behind him—but nothing.

FOUR

>>———+—————➤

Cars whizzed by as Riley stood on the side of the freeway checking his wallet for the number to his insurance company. He was pretty sure he had roadside assistance as part of the package, but where he was going to have his loaded Jeep hauled off to—he had no clue. Which meant he'd do what any capable, eighteen-year-old guy would do.

He'd call his mom.

To his relief, she answered on the first ring. "Hey, bud."

"Hi Mom." A diesel truck growled by, trailed by a cop with its siren on.

"Where are you, Riles?" She used his actual name, alarm sharp in her voice.

"Um, I'm on the side of the 10 freeway. Just outside of Palm Springs."

"Are you all right?"

"I'm fine. Everything's fine. My Jeep just died. It's

on the shoulder and I'm fine." There was this truth of the universe that the more you told your mom you were fine, the less she would believe you. So why he said it three times, he didn't know.

"Do you need to be picked up?"

"Uh…I'm not sure. I just…" He gripped the back of his neck and turned away from the road, but still felt like he was shouting. "I'm headed to Taos. Did you get my message?"

"Just got it and I'm so sorry to hear about Becca's dad."

"Thanks."

"And you're really heading out of state?"

"Yeah. I'll explain it all better, but right now I just need to figure out where I'm gonna have this towed. It needs a new tranny, but I'm not sure how long that will take." New Mexico suddenly felt like a long ways away. "Can you come and get me?"

"Honey, I'm in San Francisco at the championships. Remember I told you to put it on your calendar that I would be out of town?"

Right. Because he totally had a calendar and kept it up to date. "Ah, I forgot about that."

"We'll be done on Thursday, unless the girls make

the finals, which are on Friday…"

Riley skidded his shoe over some gravel as she talked on—to herself mostly. He could practically see her with her golden skin, worry shadowing her almond-shaped eyes. She was the best problem solver he knew, and if anyone could help him out of this bind, it'd be her.

"What about your boss?" she asked. "Or one of your friends around there? I know he lives down in Point Loma, but did you call Ramsey?"

Riley thought of his buddy who usually spent the weekend with a camera in hand. "No. I think he's shooting a wedding or something today. Besides, it'd be a far drive for him. And I don't want to bug Mr. Lawrence again. He just did me a big favor. I could maybe call Keith—" Did he know someone who had nothing to do on a Saturday?

"Riley?"

"Yeah?"

"Have you thought about calling your father? He's in Dana Point, which is a straight shot over to the 10. He could be there in a couple hours."

"How do you know he's in Dana Point?" Why did Riley not know this and what the heck was she thinking suggesting he call his dad? He hadn't called his dad since he was eleven.

"I know because I spoke with him a week ago—"

"You *spoke* with him?"

"Yes, honey, I have to do that from time to time." Her voice was kind. "Recently we had to figure out a few things now that you're eighteen. Listen, Riley, he's not far from there and I know he would love for you to call him."

"You know, Mom. This isn't the greatest time for a family reunion."

"I'm going to text you his number—"

"Mom, don't—"

Click.

Did she just…hang up on him? "Are you there?" Riley ran a hand down his face. For crying out loud. His phone beeped a moment later, her texting him some number he didn't recognize.

Once, when he got expelled in junior high for fighting again, his mom had cried to the school counselor what a handful Riley had been and how it was only getting worse. The counselor had told her to try the tough love approach, and she'd spent the rest of his life getting way too good at it.

His phone beeped again. *Do you have the number to your insurance company?*

Grinding his teeth, Riley texted back. *I got it.*

He yanked out his insurance card and dialed the 800 number. After ten minutes with the operator, he had a tow truck lined up. That's when he realized that numbers were playing a trick on his mind. Riley checked the digits his mom had sent him and compared them to the caller who'd been trying to get ahold of him.

Not possible.

An hour later, Riley was still leaning against the guardrail, sweating in the Palm Desert sun. Traffic whizzed by so loud and fast he had a headache. He had the number memorized now and had thought of all the things he wanted to say to his dad. How much he hated him. How he'd ruined his life. What the guy had done to his ex-wife and what a jerk he was.

Riley's thumb actually hovered over the keypad when he saw the tow truck pulling up. He pocketed his cell, then signed papers while the driver hooked chains to the Jeep and hauled it onto the flatbed.

Riley's phone buzzed. *Did you call him?*

No, mom.

A minute later it buzzed again and Riley yanked out his phone, ready to tell his mom to just give him a *minute* to think when he saw that it was from the Fletchers, which meant it was Becca.

How are you doing? Are you on the road yet? I'm so excited to see you. Mom and the kids are excited too. They're already talking about where you're going to sleep. Sammy offered his bunk and he's dying to show you the park we're next to. Eight-year-olds don't quite mind sleeping in a Walmart parking lot. :O) Oh my gosh, New Mexico is freezing at night so that generator is going to be AMAZING. Text me when you can. Drive safe. Can't WAIT to see you!!

Riley ran his thumb over her words.

"Ready?"

He shook his head, only to realize that the tow truck driver was staring at him.

"You getting in or do you plan on setting up camp here?" The man asked.

Walking around the hefty cab, Riley climbed up into the passenger side and slammed the door. He buckled in and rubbed his eyes with the palms of his hands. The air conditioning blasted from the vents and he tugged at the front of his shirt.

"Gotta love January in the desert." The driver climbed up. "Nearest auto shop?"

"Yeah."

"There's one a couple exits down." The guy said it like a question.

"Um, that's great, thanks. I just…" Riley pulled out his phone and with the number still fresh on his mind, punched the first half of it in. "Just need to make a call." His thumb shook a little, and before he could change his mind, he made himself dial the last four digits.

His stomach knotted as he lifted the phone to his ear and it rang.

He was going to be sick…

"Hello?" a man said. The single word was spoken cool and deep—Hawaiian.

"Dad?" Riley blurted, wondering if the guy would recognize his voice or not.

It was silent for a moment. "Who is this?"

Riley knew that while not medically possible, there were moments in life when the heart felt like it stopped. "It's me. Riley."

"Riles?"

"Yeah."

Dead silence.

"Dad?" Riley leaned his elbow on the door, really wishing he wasn't having this conversation in front of someone else. "You there?"

"I'm here," Jake Kane blurted quickly. "H—how are you doing?"

Riley scratched the back of his head. "Uh, *great*."

"What's...what's up?" His dad quickly said something to someone in the background and Riley could tell he only had half of his attention. "Say, hang on just a sec, Riles."

Riley rolled his eyes.

His dad must have turned away from the phone because he spoke to whoever was there.

You know what? Who cared if he burdened his dad? He was officially committed to asking for a ride. In fact, he kind of wished gas was made out of solid gold right now.

"You still there?"

"Yeah. I need a ride. My Jeep broke down and I'm on the 10 in Palm Desert. Mom said to call you." He didn't mean to throw her under the bus on that one, but he wanted to make sure to clarify that this wasn't exactly voluntary. "I don't mind staying in a hotel, but she said you might be able to come get me." And with transmission trouble and his not-so-big savings, he didn't know how he was going to get his truck running again.

"Uh...yeah. I can come get you. I can actually leave

right now."

Really? That was way too easy. Switching his phone to the other ear, Riley asked the driver for the address to the auto shop, and after relaying it, his dad promised to be there in less than two hours. With an awkward goodbye, they hung up.

Leaning back against the seat that smelled like oil and air fresheners, Riley shoved all worries off his dad and thought of Becca and the kids freezing in that Walmart parking lot. Was it even safe where they were? He hated that they were alone so far from home. The thought of seeing if his dad could give him a ride out there or lend him a car or something came, but Riley decided to zip his lips on that one and see how the next couple of hours played out. With his luck, his dad probably wouldn't even show.

FIVE

Sitting outside the repair shop's office, Riley leaned forward and rested his elbows on his knees. With his duffle bag between his shoes, he watched the road, even though he had no idea what kind of car his father drove. Was he supposed to call him Dad? Or Jake?

He couldn't decide right now, especially while fighting a headache. After a granola bar and a bottle of water, he wasn't starving anymore, but something about the noise and fumes of the freeway had wedged at the base of his temples in an ache that he couldn't rub away.

The nearest stoplight turned from red to green, and a few seconds later an old VW van pulled into the parking lot of the auto shop. Riley squinted beneath the afternoon sun. The what-used-to-be-turquoise van parked. A few seconds later, the door creaked open. A man dressed in jeans and skater shoes climbed out. His skin was golden brown, slicked-back hair jet black—all traits of a Hawaiian heritage. Riley's skin was lighter, but for crying out loud, did they have to look so much alike?

His dad wore a plain white tee and slipped on designer sunglasses before glancing around. He spotted Riley and froze. Still on the bench, Riley straightened.

His heart was in his stomach again.

With one hand shoved in the pocket of his jeans, the man started toward him. "Riley?"

Swallowing a crummy feeling in his chest, Riley stood slowly. "Yeah." Was the guy going to try and hug him or something?

But he just said, "Man, you're tall."

Which meant sarcasm was about to get the best of him. "I'm only five nine, Pop."

"The last time I saw you, you were…"

"Three feet?"

The smile creases around Jake Kane's eyes faded and the man looked away a moment. Then he glanced to Riley's duffle bag and backpack. "You ready to go, or do we need to take care of anything inside?" His voice held that deep, earthy sound that only Islanders had.

"I just need to get some stuff out of my Jeep. Could you drive over to the back?"

"You got it."

Riley headed around the stucco building to the open

garage where his truck was parked off to the side, no doubt waiting its turn in line. He didn't even want to think about a new transmission right now. He wanted to go take a shower, then call the mechanic later and see what the damage would be. When the VW backed up to it, Riley lifted the van's hatch and noticed that the third row seat had been taken out. Which worked out perfect as he switched the lighter stuff—some bedding, the jugs and gas cans—to the other vehicle. His dad opened the side doors and set Riley's backpack in.

"Mind helping me lift this?" Riley gripped one side of the generator.

Jake moved to clear some of his own things out of the way. With a *1-2-3*, they lifted the generator up into the back opening, just above the engine compartment.

"Thanks." Riley brushed his hands on his pants, not quite looking up.

It took him only a minute to move the rest of his gear. When his dad latched the back hatch, Riley took a final glance at his poor Jeep, then climbed into the Volkswagen. The interior was a weird green color and it smelled like coconuts. Talk radio rambled soft from the speakers. And here he had expected the Beach Boys.

His dad hit the power on the radio and the car went

quiet.

"Thanks for picking me up," Riley made himself say as his dad put the van into gear.

"No problem."

Sure.

"We should be to my place by four. You hungry?"

"I'm fine."

"Okay. We can grab a bite in Dana Point. There's a nice little shrimp shack I think you'll like."

Riley drew a slow breath. "I'm allergic to shellfish."

His dad blinked out the windshield for a few moments. He hit his blinker to merge onto the freeway. "That's right. I forgot." He glanced out his side mirror and veered into the left lane. "Burgers?"

Riley stared out his window. "That's fine."

Jake was quiet for a little while. "Do you carry one of those things with you? In case you have a reaction to something? Do I need to know anything about it?"

"An EpiPen? I have one in my bag. I know how to do it."

His dad shot out a slow sigh, then changed lanes again.

Riley folded his arms across his middle, leaned his head against the rest, and wished he was home. Better yet, with Becca. In the Fletchers' tiny trailer, eating pretzels and peanut butter like he had the other night when they'd watched *Elf* side by side on the sofa. Maybe that was a stupid wish, but it was easy and safe. The world wasn't really complicated then.

Or maybe it was. Maybe he couldn't get away from all of this no matter how hard he tried, because he could still remember the feel of Becca's fingers as she'd pushed his hair off to the side and peered closely at him...then asked the one question he hated answering.

She'd been telling a few funny stories about her father, neither she nor Riley paying as much attention to the movie as the little ones were. Ten-year-old Tyler had fallen asleep with his head in Becca's lap. The blinking lights from the neighbor's trailer had lit her face as she asked Riley when the last time he saw his dad was.

Riley had scratched his head and quipped something about a recent magazine featuring the '50 Most Beautiful People in the World.' *"My dad was number twenty-nine and I'm still grossed out."*

Becca had giggled, but the sincerity in her eyes pulled him back to the real question at hand.

Knowing he couldn't dodge it, Riley had cleared his throat. *"I haven't seen him since I was in third grade."*

She'd looked at him then. Sadly.

"Got a girlfriend?" his dad's voice snapped him back to the present.

Riley glanced at the man in the driver's seat. Jake's slicked-back hair caught the light streaming in, and a high-end watch wrapped the tanned wrist that draped the steering wheel.

Riley rested one of his shoes on top of the other. "Do *you*?"

"No."

His dad looked out his side window. Riley did the same. He didn't feel like talking, so he rested an elbow on the door frame and leaned the side of his head against the glass. The AC kit worked okay, but the van still felt claustrophobic. He sat there, thinking of all the different ways he hated this and all the different ways he was going to try and get home—or get to Becca—when his dad asked him where he was headed.

"New Mexico." When the guy's eyebrows shot up, Riley continued. "The gear in the back is for some friends of mine. A family. It's a mom and some kids. The dad's in the hospital in Taos and they're staying in a trailer and needed some extra stuff, so I was going to take it out there."

"That's good of you."

"Yeah. Well…" Riley stared out the window again. "Didn't exactly get very far."

The vehicle lurched along with a shift to fourth. The speedometer rose closer to fifty and everything rattled.

"Is this thing safe?" Riley asked as he eyed the dash of what he knew to be one of the rarest VW's in existence.

The surfer's mouth quirked up. "She'll hold. Hasn't failed me yet."

"'65?"

His dad glanced at him for the briefest of moments. "How'd you know that?"

"Just a lucky guess. They didn't make microbuses with twenty-one windows until 1964, and it's too junky for a '66."

To Riley's surprise, his dad chuckled.

He hadn't meant to be funny. Not really wanting to have a father-son bonding moment, Riley pulled out a set of headphones—the sound-canceling Bose that his mom got him for Christmas. He slipped them into place, then hit play on his iPod, not caring what he listened to, as long as he could escape. He closed his eyes. The bump of the van as it careened toward the coast mixed with the sun pouring in through the glass made him tired enough to fall asleep, so he had to keep shifting his feet to stay awake.

After a while, a tap on his arm made him sit up straighter and pull off his headphones.

"Do you care what kind of burgers we grab?" his dad asked.

"Anything's fine."

They went another few miles before hitting an exit. The speedometer lowered, and away from the noise of the freeway, Riley slid open the window, getting his first blast of sea air. It was heavy and salty and made him think of some of the worst days of his life. But he breathed it deeply for some reason, letting it clear his head. *Poor man's coffee*, his dad used to call it. Riley watched the horizon move by.

Palm trees stood tall in patches and shrubs lined the road where they pulled into town. A gas station, a homeless man on a bicycle, two kids skating down the sidewalk on longboards. A black Ford with a surfboard in the back.

Dana Point.

This was the town he was born in. The town his dad had left them in.

Leaning back against his seat, Riley propped the

soles of his shoes on the dash and watched it all pass by. When his dad cleared his throat a little too loudly, Riley pulled his Converse back to the floor. With a clink of the blinker, the van turned left into an In-N-Out Burger, and his stomach grumbled for the salty fries and a root beer.

Jake parked and they climbed out. Riley shoved his hands in his pockets and they walked in silence up to the building. His dad held the door open for him. Riley made an *after you* motion with his hand, then trailed him into the burger joint that was the lifeblood to pretty much any west coaster. The twenty-something girl at the cash register stared wide eyed as his dad walked up to the counter and ordered a Double-Double Animal style. Riley asked her for a cheeseburger with extra pickles.

Two fries. Two root beers.

His dad's accent was strong. Riley had forgotten just how much. Then again, maybe it was fake. Some smooth way to get along with the ladies. As it was, the girl taking their order looked about to faint as she handed the surfer his change. Jake flashed a million-dollar smile and she blushed.

Riley rolled his eyes and pulled out his wallet. His dad told him to put it away, so Riley carried the tray over to a table. He sat while Jake went for ketchup and napkins. A few patrons glanced that way. Several others whispered with surprised expressions.

Remembering he hadn't texted Becca back, Riley slipped out his phone.

Hey, Becca. I had some car trouble so it's in the shop. My dad picked me up and I'm gonna figure out what to do next. I'm so sorry that things got messed up. I still have all of your things and I'm going to figure out a way to get everything to you.

He took a deep breath then added, *Miss you.* A lot.

The bright, '50s-red chair across from him creaked as his dad sat. Jake dumped out his fries onto the wax paper from his burger, then added salt. Riley did the same. He ate in silence, downing half of his soda in a few gulps. His phone beeped and he tapped the screen.

Oh. WOW. I'm so sorry! Are you alright? Call me when you can. Miss you too.

Becca added a little heart and Riley smiled.

"You never answered my question," his dad said before cramming two fries into his mouth. "Girlfriend?" he mumbled, eying the screen with its lit-up text.

Riley slid his phone farther from the tray and took a bite of his burger. "She's not my girlfriend," he mumbled back. "I had to tell her I got hung up."

"She in that family? That you're taking the stuff to?"

"Yeah." Riley ate, more interested in his food than the man across from him.

His dad reached toward the phone. "Well, if she's not your girlfriend, what's the heart for—"

Riley back-handed his reach away and the guy looked genuinely hurt.

"*Just* teasing…"

"Well I don't want to be teased, all right?" Riley took another bite of his food, wishing they could eat at separate tables. His anger-management counselor would tell him to count to ten. Pastor Keith would have told him to take a deep breath—think of something he was thankful for. Instead, he ate fast enough to make himself sick, then headed out without excusing himself.

Riley stood in the parking lot beside the van, staring at the sky until a pair of guys walked by. One of them pulled out a camera to take a picture of the Volkswagen. Riley rolled his eyes, and even though he'd called the van junky, knew that it was so rare a model, a new paint job would put it over a hundred grand. The pair walked away and Riley tapped his shoe against one of the tires.

Jake came out a few minutes later, two sodas in hand. He held one of the cups out without a word. Riley didn't take it.

"Should I just throw it in the trash?"

When Riley didn't answer, his dad set the red and white cup on the pavement beside the van. He started toward the driver's side, then halted and turned. Still palming his own drink, he lifted a thick finger to point at Riley. "You know what? I don't know why I'm putting up with this. You're just a punk kid."

"And you're just a *jerk* dad." Riley straightened, seriously ready for a fight.

His dad shifted his jaw, then adjusted his silver watch. "What am I even doing here with you?" He clamped his mouth closed—as if regretting that.

Riley just stared at him, wondering what the superstar would look like with a broken nose. "I hear they needed a runner-up for *Dad of the Year*."

"I called you—"

"And it was ten years too late."

Setting his mouth, Jake looked off in the distance. A little boy screeched as he skipped out of the fast food joint and swung up on his grandpa's arm. Jake dipped his head, rattled the keys in his hand, then looked back at Riley. "Just get in the van."

"Thanks. I think I'll walk home."

"Knock yourself out." He stepped around to the driver's side. "I'll stash all this stuff in my garage until you come and get it." He climbed in and slammed his door.

Dang it.

The engine rumbled to life and Riley glimpsed everything filling the back of the van. Gritting his teeth, he slowly opened his own door. He took a moment to breathe deeply before climbing in. He buckled and his dad backed out without a word.

SIX

In the parking spot in front of an apartment building, Riley didn't look at his dad until he killed the engine and pocketed the keys—making no move to exit. The engine clicked as it cooled.

Jake unbuckled, not looking up. "Now what?"

Riley rubbed at his forehead, completely lost. "I have no idea."

"You need to get back home, I'd imagine."

Riley shifted his feet. "I need to get to New Mexico."

As if lost in thought, his dad took his sweet time opening the driver's side door. "Well." He sat back against the seat again. "I've got contacts pretty much everywhere. Let's go inside and I'll make a few calls."

There was something about the easy way he said it that made Riley feel worse.

When Jake climbed out, Riley went around and hefted his stuff from the back. Hitching the thick canvas strap over his shoulder, Riley followed him up a flight of stairs. The apartment building didn't exactly say rich-n-famous, but it was nicer than most. It even had a garage. Why the VW didn't get parked in there was beyond him. A fountain trickled in the courtyard behind them, and Riley stopped when his dad paused at a tall white door and slid a key into the lock. He palmed the door open and Riley stepped past.

Still outside the faintly-lit entry, Jake slipped out of his skate shoes. He set them on a rack beside the door.

That's right. It was the Hawaiian way. Feeling like a punk, Riley stepped back and took off his own shoes. After the lights were flicked on, he was met with white tile floors, white walls, and a few potted palms in the living room. The biggest flat screen he'd ever seen hung over a modern-style fireplace. Couches as bright as everything else looked like they had never been sat on.

As if answering some unspoken question, his dad said, "I'm just renting this for a few months." He tossed his keys on a tall, polished table. "Make yourself at home."

Riley stood in the entryway, duffle strap on his shoulder—having no idea how to go about that.

His dad folded his sunglasses before pocketing them. "Uh...I guess we should nail down some specifics. I'll make a couple calls. And in the meantime, I'll show you to a room and you can get comfortable. Shower if you want…whatever. There's bottled water in the fridge and you can help yourself to anything you need. I'll order a pizza or something later. Once we figure out how to get you on your way, we'll have a better idea of things. But for now…" he looked at Riley, "make yourself comfortable."

Riley nodded once, not really sure what to say to any of that. Especially after the words they'd swapped outside the burger joint. "Okay."

Jake led him upstairs to a hallway. On the right Riley spotted what looked like a game room. It had a pool table in the center and autographed surfboards leaned against the wall. His eyes slid from those to a bookshelf covered with gaming controls. Nice.

At the next room, his dad opened the door and motioned in. "This one has a bathroom. I'm sure you've got all your stuff, but if you need anything, just ask. Or you're welcome to use the van. Also, the cleaning lady comes on Monday. I'll try and give you a heads up if you're still here." He stepped out of the room and Riley heard him head back down the hallway.

Riley set down his bag, then rubbed at the ache in his

shoulder while he checked out the bathroom. That didn't take long, and a minute later he found himself sitting on the double bed, feet squared, eyes on the far wall.

From below, his dad seemed to be speaking to someone on the phone. Riley heard his name once…and then again. Not really wanting to sit around, he pulled out his own phone and shot a message to his mom to tell her that he was safe and where he was. She replied a few seconds later.

I'm proud of you.

Riley stared at those words—wondering what she was so proud of. He'd just called his dad a jerk and would say worse if pressed. He tossed his phone in the center of the bed, and dipping his head, ran his hands into his hair, holding them there.

His parents were on speaking terms? How did he miss this?

With nothing else to do—and sick of feeling like he was covered in freeway exhaust—Riley took a shower and put on some fresh clothes. He even brushed his teeth out of sheer boredom. As he slid into socks, he thought of his dad's game room, but wasn't really ready to wander around. He was just zipping up the clear gallon bag he had stashed his toiletries in when there was a knock at the door.

Riley opened it to find his dad standing there, one hand in a pocket, the other hand gripping his phone. "So I have a few options."

"Okay."

"There's this guy I know who's heading that way. South—I think he said Brazil. He's got a Cessna. Do you know what that is?"

"It's a plane."

"Yeah. He's leaving in a couple hours for a film he's working on and can adjust his flight to drop you off pretty close to the spot. As long as it's okay that you ride back with your friends when they come home. Problem is, the pilot's got a bunch of camera gear with him so you wouldn't be able to bring all that stuff with you. But it would get you there. Probably even sometime tonight."

Tonight. Becca's face flashed through his mind. And a plane? That was awesome.

"Of course, there's the good old-fashioned plane ticket which we could buy you instead. Airport's not far from here. Same problem, though—kinda hard to check a generator and a bunch of old water jugs."

"Right."

"Another option is this." He sighed, and leaning

against the doorjamb, looked straight at Riley, then down to his feet. "I'm heading up to Northern California to meet up with a buddy of mine who lives there. We're doing a tournament together in Texas on the Gulf. We were gonna work on some things at his place, then fly out together. Tickets are all set."

Riley scratched the back of his head, having no idea what this had to do with him.

"I just got off the phone with him as well. His name's Saul. One thing you and I could do…is head up to his place as planned, and then all start off toward Texas in my van. We'll have all your stuff that way. I'd say— tops—we'd be to New Mexico in a couple of days. Saul and I can drop you off then head to the Gulf. I'd just have to call the airport and see about cashing the tickets in."

Riley stared at his dad. There was no way he'd just heard him right.

After a few seconds, the side of Jake's mouth tipped up. "Do I need to say all that again or are you still in there somewhere?"

Riley blinked and quick-shook his head. "Uh…sorry. Just thinking. Um…" He squinted. "Maybe you should say it again."

To his surprise, Jake laughed a little, then he repeated

himself, filling in a few more details about his buddy with the single-engine Cessna.

Riley held up a hand. "I mean the part about taking your van."

"Oh." Jake—Dad—or whatever he was supposed to call him—leaned against the doorjamb again and crossed his ankles. "Well...I guess..." he shrugged. "I don't know. I just...if you need to get there, and you need to get that stuff there, then it seems to make the most sense."

Riley stared at him.

Because an eight-year-old needing his dad apparently *hadn't* made sense.

Mouth suddenly dry, Riley wet his lips. "Uh... okay. If you want to." He didn't know how to say thank you. Had no clue. Those words wouldn't form—not if he were to mean them. For the Fletchers' sake, though, he wanted to say something. "Taking everything in the van—that will be good for the family. I appreciate it."

His dad nodded a little. "No problem. I'll make those calls and we'll be squared away." He glanced around as if not knowing what to say next. "Got everything you need?"

"Yeah."

"Want to play a game of pool or something when I'm

done?"

"No thanks."

"Wanna watch some TV?"

"Not really."

Jake glanced at the ground then pressed the pad of his thumb across his lips. "All right then. I'll leave you to take it easy." He started down the hall.

Riley watched him go. When the guy halted and glanced back, Riley took a step into the hall. But his dad just told him to let him know when he got hungry. Riley nodded.

When he was gone, Riley couldn't bring himself to sit anymore, so he found the game room again. He peered in and glanced around before walking over to the surfboards. Because they were signed, he wasn't sure if he was supposed to touch them or not, but he gently ran his fingertip over some of the signatures on a vintage longboard. He recognized several names from surfing magazines and the competitions he used to watch as a kid.

"When is Dad gonna be on?" he'd ask.

His mom would look at him, her brow creased with worry, then hand him the remote. *"Riley. Are you sure you want to watch it?"*

Was she kidding? He couldn't tune in to the sports

channel fast enough. He was nine then—still under the impression that his dad's *gotta go* was a temporary arrangement.

He'd settle on the couch, popcorn in his lap, and cheer whenever his dad was announced over the loud-speaker. Then Riley would sit on edge and watch the heat begin. His favorite part—when the surfers first paddled into the swell. He could still remember the time his dad got a 10.0 when he blew out of a fifteen-footer after a perfect barrel. Riley had jumped up on the couch, spilling popcorn everywhere, and cheered at the top of his lungs.

His mom just watched from the kitchen, arms folded around her waist.

Years later, when Riley hadn't heard from his father in a couple of years, a boy from his math class had shown him that Jake Kane had signed his skateboard while on vacation in Santa Monica. Riley had told the eighth grader to go jump off a cliff. A few punches and a crushed trash can later, they were both in the principal's office; the kid with a busted-up lip and Riley across the hall from him using his shirt to stop a bloody nose. A few feet away, his mom had cried to the counselor about being overwhelmed.

And now his dad wanted to play pool.

SEVEN

When Becca had said he could write her a letter if he wanted, she probably didn't know he'd never written one in his life. Or that his spelling was a nightmare. On the bed, legs folded in, Riley held the notepad he'd packed and stared at the blank paper. He set the spiral book in his lap and uncapped the pen. "Horrendous" described his handwriting, so he tried to go slowly. Across the first line, then the second. He paused and chewed the end of the cap. If he was going to say all this, he wanted to do it well, and like a dummy, he hadn't thought to bring a pencil. Something he could erase. This letter wasn't going to have a whole lot of do overs.

Kind of like his life.

But there were *try agains,* and that's why he wanted to do this—with Becca—right.

If they were going to become any kind of *us*…he had to. He'd lived so much life out of order, especially when it came to past girlfriends. He meant to forget them in his room and the dark—but like pen, he could only cross things out. Black it all into oblivion. But it would never really be gone. And Becca's heart was marked because of that.

He wrote a whole *half page* before his hand got unsteady. He could text a million miles a minute, but this was totally different. Setting the notebook aside, he'd add to it before bed. And now he was trying not to think about the girls he owed a few words to. He could spare the sheets of paper, but writing any of that...getting it to them...

Suddenly overwhelmed, Riley capped his pen. He headed downstairs to where his dad was on the phone again. Riley poked around the living area, looking at some of the DVDs lining the wall. When the doorbell rang, he saw through the sheer curtains a pizza delivery guy. Riley opened the door and fished out his wallet, trading twenty-five bucks for the two hot boxes.

He carried everything over to the counter as his dad talked on—seemingly to the airline, because he was discussing dates and refunds. Always hungry, Riley peeked inside the first pizza box to find the golden-brown cheese covered with pepperoni and black olives. The second—Canadian bacon and pineapple. His dad pulled paper plates from the pantry and handed them to Riley. Phone between ear and shoulder, Jake listened to whoever was helping him. At the fridge, he pulled out two beers.

When he handed one out, Riley propped a fist on the counter and pulled cheese off his slice with his other hand. "Please tell me you know what year I was born."

"Oh...right." He set the second can on the counter and popped the metal top on his own. Riley checked the fridge, then nabbed a bottle of water. He settled on a stool at the tiled bar.

By the time he polished off his first piece of pizza, his dad finished his phone call.

"Okay. Tickets are all squared away and I was able to get credit with the airline." He took a slice of pepperoni with olives, then settled on one of the cushioned barstools beside Riley. "I spoke to Saul and he's cool with us leaving earlier than planned, which means..." he bit into his pizza and spoke around the bite, "we're good to leave in the morning." He ran a napkin over his mouth, then swigged from the can.

"Cool."

They ate in silence for a while and Riley knew he needed to make an effort. At the very least, a thank you. The words left his lips as he sat looking at his food and his dad said, "You're welcome," doing the same.

When they finished eating, his dad tried to pay him for the pizzas, but Riley refused. He didn't want any handouts. The rest of the pizza went into the fridge and his dad wiped down the counters with a sponge, looking surprisingly domestic. Riley had always imagined the athlete would have someone to pay to do that kind of stuff for him.

With a night sky glittering through the front windows, Riley grabbed his shoes and took his cell out the back door to the apartment complex's inner courtyard. Overhead lights brightened the space. The fountain bubbled nearby while he slipped on his shoes then he settled down on an iron chair near the Jacuzzi. He dialed Becca, hoping she'd be able to accept his FaceTime request.

The phone rang a couple times. Suddenly his screen came to life with the top half of Mrs. Fletcher's twisted, brown and silver bun. The woman punched buttons, asking Becca how to get it to work. Becca appeared in the other half of the screen, as if to see if it was working yet.

Riley could hardly contain his joy. "Hi!"

"Oh my gosh, it's on!" Becca cried and nearly klunked heads with her mom while they tried to get the phone to line up straight. Suddenly it was just Becca. "Can you see me okay?"

Riley grinned so big his face hurt. "Perfectly."

Becca grinned right back. "It's you!" Her hair was braided in a crown across her head—all wispy and golden brown with the porch light streaming in through the trailer window behind her. She wore a pair of earrings he knew she'd made. His real-life Gypsy.

"How are you?" He leaned forward, careful to hold his phone steady. "*I miss you.*"

Her eyes were bright and filled with the same gentle wonder he remembered from the day they met. "I miss you too." She said it in a whisper. Like a wish.

For there not to be miles upon miles between them.

"How's your dad doing?" he asked.

The light in her eyes faded. "He still hasn't woken up. He's gone through two surgeries already and has one more scheduled first thing in the morning." She pulled the phone closer, then pushed it back, trying to get her face centered on the screen for him.

"I'm so sorry. How's your mom holding up?"

Becca craned her neck. Her mom was probably outside. "She's doing okay. She's really strong. But it's hard." She peered back down at the screen. "We don't know what's going to happen. I got to see him and he looked terrible. The accident was really bad."

Was it best to ask for more details? Or would that cause her pain?

She continued before he needed to decide.

"His semi flipped and the firefighters had to cut the cab apart to get him out. The mom who was driving the minivan—the one who swerved when she saw the deer—said she was sure they were going to be crushed when she looked up and saw my dad's semi. But that suddenly he was just gone and the whole trailer was flying into a ditch. Even the firefighters didn't know how he could have turned the truck that hard and fast, but he did."

Becca wiped at her eyes. The connection wobbled, a flash of white moved past, and she settled back with a tissue in hand.

His voice felt weak. "How are the kids holding up?"

"They're doing well. Anna said the sweetest prayer for my dad before eating tonight. It was actually a candy bar, which made it all the more precious. My mom started crying all over again and I did too. We've become the 'girls who cry.'" Becca waved her tissue to make her point and Riley smiled gently the same instant she did.

"Is it still freezing?" he asked.

"I had no idea a place like New Mexico could be so cold at night. I always thought it was just the desert." She dabbed at her eyes again. "We've always run our heater in the trailer so never had to worry about being cold back at home, but without power…it's *kinda chilly.* We got some extra blankets and one of the nurses from the hospital even got us set up with some donations from her church. She's super nice. Oh, and I think we might even be going to a nearby campground. It will be a farther drive to the hospital, but they have hookups."

"That would be awesome."

"Oh! And I got my own phone!" She said it in a sing-song voice, then sniffed again. "It's just a pre-paid phone, but with my mom going to the hospital by herself sometimes, she thought it would be a good idea for me to have. The plan says I can text all I want. She's still going to check it, though," she added a little shyly, then gave him her number.

"I would expect nothing less." And he didn't blame the woman one bit. Riley wet his lips—thinking of what they'd talked about the other night. He tried to think of something to say, some comfort, but Becca spoke first.

"And what about you? Tell me about your dad. How's all that going?"

"I'm…" He blinked a second. "I'm doing good. It's going…good."

"I've been thinking about you two together. I'm so amazed. And proud of you."

Just like his mom.

He wanted to smile because there was something about the arrangement with his dad that should have filled him with a new energy, but he just felt drained in a way he couldn't describe. He felt a peace and a warmth when he was with Becca—like right now—but when she was gone, so was that feeling. The feeling of being in the right place. Of being safe. But that seemed way too deep for FaceTime, so he just assured her that it was going okay. "He's actually gonna drive me out there, so I'll be to New Mexico in a couple days, and I still have all your gear."

She grinned. "*Really*? That's so nice of him! I can't wait to see you. And now I get to meet your dad."

"You've wanted to meet my dad?" Never a rare thing with him and friends, but with Becca he knew it was different. She wasn't out to get anything signed.

"Well…" Her expression went soft. "He's your dad. I'm excited to meet your mom, too. Both of your parents."

"Really?" No one ever cared that he had a mom.

"Of course." In her eyes there was a touch of sorrow

as if she understood. "Are you sure you're doing okay?"

"Honestly, I'm okay." Riley glanced to the fountain where two moths fluttered around the water. "To answer your question…it's going fine. It's just temporary anyway and he's not that bad to be around."

"I really hope you guys have a good couple of days."

"That's what my mom would say."

Becca winked and her face made him think of home. "Hang in there…" Eyes wide and searching, she went quiet. Just looking at him in a way that shot right to his heart. "I miss you," she said again.

Riley ran a hand over his chest. "Me too."

She smiled and then chaos erupted around her. Wherever the kids had been, they'd just gotten back because it was a scuffle of noise and jostling little people. And was that a Nerf football flying across the trailer? Becca screeched and ducked. "I better go, but I'll see you in a couple of days." She waved then ducked again. "I can't wait. Oh! And I'm drawing up some t-shirts for you. I'll show you when you get here. *Drive safe* and thank you so much. Please keep in touch."

"You got it." He wanted to say more, some endearment, but he didn't know what fit. So he sealed her face in his mind, and something in his chest burned as he said a goodbye. She gave another cheery wave then tapped her fingertip to the screen. She must have thought that shut it off, because she set the phone down and rose. Though the angle was now lopsided, Riley could see her lift a folded blanket off the sofa and drape it out.

She asked whose turn it was for the couch. CJ said it was Becca's, but Tyler popped up from the dinette asking if he could have it. The kid was wearing a jacket...inside.

"The floor is sooo cold," Tyler said. "I almost froze last night."

Riley knew this wasn't his scene to see, but he couldn't move. Couldn't look away. Because the next second, Becca tilted her head to the side, flashed her little brother that dimpled smile, then said, "Rock, paper, scissors."

One...two...

Tyler put down scissors, and with her hand lowering in a winning fist, Becca quickly opened her fingers, slamming down a palm. Paper.

Losing.

Chills covered Riley's skin. His brow dipped and he watched as Becca kissed her brother on the top of the head. Tyler flung himself onto the sofa. Riley tapped his phone, sending the screen to black. He shouldn't have even watched that much.

He thought the bed was Becca's. Thought she always slept there. She took turns? And even gave hers up for her brother? Lowering his head, Riley used his thumb and forefinger to rub at his forehead.

When a maintenance guy walked over to the Jacuzzi and gathered up a pair of forgotten towels, Riley made himself rise. It was too early to go to bed, so maybe he'd just hang around his dad's apartment for another hour then go to bed.

He went in the back door and walked through the kitchen. He took his time looking at the few pictures hanging on the wall of the living room. A few black and white portraits of his dad and his friends surfing. A vintage shot of a woman in a Hawaiian dress with a thick lei around her neck. Though the old photo was grainy, Riley recognized the shot of his grandmother. He had a smaller version of the same picture stashed somewhere in a box of stuff from when he was a kid. Her name was Ailani. Full- blooded Hawaiian, she looked the part, standing there barefoot with the sea behind her and its breeze pushing her long black hair to one side.

Riley didn't have any photos of his grandfather. The man—a fisherman—had died at sea not long after having a son. That's all he'd learned from his mom. Maybe all she knew herself.

Riley moved to the next picture which was a print of the sea. A calm, quiet, gray sea. Not the kind one often saw around the surfing world. In the center of the print was small, square text:

live in the sunshine.

swim the sea.

drink the wild air.

– Emerson

Riley touched the frame of the print, glanced once more at the grandma he met a few times as a baby, then peeled his gaze away from the past and headed through the hallway. There weren't any pictures of him and that was just fine.

Down a dim set of stairs he heard a soft clanking on the other side of the door at the bottom. He had a hunch it was the garage, and when he opened it, saw Jake standing at a workbench with a new skateboard deck in front of him. About to add grip tape by the looks of it. Riley eyed the graphics that labeled it as a deck from one of the most prestigious companies in the biz. Several other boards hung from the wall.

Jake glanced up and wiped his fingers on the side of

a faded tank. "Hey." He lifted up the sheet of sandpapery grip and peeled off the backing.

Riley didn't really want to make conversation but knew he needed to try, so he walked over. "Nice board."

"Thanks. I thought I'd throw it on top of the van. Maybe you can break it in for me. You still ride?"

"Sometimes."

His dad eyed him.

"There's a park where I live which is pretty impressive for a town like that. It's not great, but I can teach the kids tricks. Nearly broke my wrist there last summer."

"*Nice.*"

"Comes with the territory." Riley pulled out a stool and sat.

"Don't I know it." His dad pressed down on the gritty, black surface, the skin of his shoulders brown and tanned. He was probably close to forty if not a year or two over, but the muscle there looked as strong as ever, reminding Riley of when he was younger and those very arms tossed him into the air.

Riley cleared his throat and adjusted the handle of a screwdriver.

"What else do you do?"

"Uh. I play the drums." Riley glanced around the tidy garage. "Used to wrestle in high school. Won a couple medals."

"I saw some pictures."

When Riley glanced back to his dad, the man's smile was kind.

"And you snowboard, too, right? Your mom said you're going later on in the winter. Where ya headed?"

"I was going to go to Utah. But that's kind of done now."

Jake looked at him with a question in his nearly-black eyes.

"New transmission and all."

"Gotcha."

Riley watched the man as he worked, still weirded out by how much they looked alike. He'd seen plenty of pictures of his dad over the years, had even watched a documentary featuring him and some of his buddies on the North Shore in Hawaii, but right now, sitting two feet from him was downright strange. The deep smile lines around his eyes told of spending years in saltwater and sun.

"I thought maybe we'd hit the road at about six in the morning. Cool with you?"

"Yeah." Riley handed his dad the razor blade that he'd need next. "How long will it take to get there? To your buddy's?"

"Saul's? About a day." Jake scraped the razor blade along the edges of the gritty paper. "Depending on if we hit traffic or not. And how many potty breaks you need."

Riley rolled his eyes. "I'll try to keep it under two. And I promise not to spill my sippy cup."

"That's my boy."

Riley's brow pinched. He peered down at the concrete floor and toed a crack with his skate shoes. Twisting his mouth to the side, he had no idea what to say to that. So he just left it where it was and rose.

Not surprised that his dad owned—and likely rode—every kind of board, Riley backtracked to the high-end skateboards and pulled one down.

Setting it to the concrete floor, he rode forward a few meters. He balanced on the balls of his feet, then shot the board up, flipping it once. He landed in a smooth roll but had to hop off before he hit the garage door. It took him three attempts to land the trick the way he liked. A bend of the knees, small wiggle to his back heel. Pop. Rotate. Land. Then he did a few 360 flips for good measure—just to up the challenge and for the familiar clang of the wheels against concrete. The garage wasn't really big enough for this, so he skidded to a stop in front of the giant door for the final time.

He gripped the deck and hung the board where he'd found it.

Jake spoke while looking at the surface of the one he was setting up. "That was some prime footwork. I think you just showed up a few pros I know."

Riley spun a wheel and then stepped away. He shoved his hands in his pockets. "Uh…like I said, not a whole lot to do where I live." And the three sponsors that he'd turned down in the last year had probably only wanted him for his name, anyway.

"Yeah, well, that was a little better than someone who was bored."

"Maybe it just runs in the genes." Riley said it flatly and moved toward the door. "I think I'm gonna head to bed."

"Need anything?"

"Nope." Riley went to step in the house.

"*Riles.*"

He turned a little.

"Look. I'm sorry about earlier. I shouldn't have called you a punk. I—" Jake glanced around. "I don't really know how to do this." He motioned between them. "So I'm probably gonna screw up a bit. Probably a lot, okay?"

"If you say so."

"Hey."

Still looking at his dad, Riley tipped his chin up, waiting.

"I don't blame you for being mad at me. I deserve it. But…if we could just get through these next couple of days in one piece, that'd be great. I have a really important week coming up and you do too. If we could just set the past aside for now…I think we'd both get to New Mexico in better shape."

Riley nodded slowly. And as he did—he felt a bit of that warmth that he felt when he was around Becca. But that made no sense because he was with his dad.

Riley looked the man square in the eye, said, "It's a deal," and for the second time that day, tried to believe that maybe he could actually get through this.

EIGHT

Boston — More Than a Feeling

Counting Crows — Mr. Jones

Seven Lions — Worlds Apart

Josh Garrels — Ulysses

Headphones in place, Riley tapped the new song in his riding mix. The way-too-early morning weighed heavy on him as he pulled up the hood of his sweatshirt and leaned his head against the passenger window of his dad's van. He closed his eyes. Sun streamed through the cool glass and he welcomed the thought of snagging another hour of sleep. It would only make it easier to deal with the fact that they were heading north, as opposed to southeast. He held onto his dad's words that they should make it to his buddy's house in about a day.

Music pumped through the headphones. The fog that lined the highway chilled the whole van so he pulled his hood farther over his forehead. Arms folded, he was just drifting off when Jake nudged him. Riley heaved out a sigh and pulled off his headphones.

"There's a map in the glove compartment. Grab it for me, will ya?"

Riley sat up a little straighter. "Like a paper map?"

The lines around his dad's eyes crinkled. "Yeah."

Riley pried open the glove compartment. He fished out the map and closed the hatch. "Haven't you ever heard of GPS?"

"Just open it. Look for San Luis Obispo."

The map accordioned to the floorboard when Riley shook it out.

"Easy!"

"*Okay!*" Riley loosened the folds of paper like museum people handled artifacts on the Discovery Channel.

"Sometime today."

Riley threw him a look. "Seriously?"

"Open the map like a grown-up and knock it off."

Despite himself, Riley chuckled. Finished, he wedged the stupid map up against the windshield, careful to keep it out of his dad's way. His finger found California and slid up the shoreline to San Luis Obispo. That's when he cocked his head to the side. Beside the city was a handwritten phone number. Beside most coastal cities were phone numbers. "Please don't tell me you have a girl in every town."

"Can it and read me the number. I need to make a call."

"It's illegal to talk on your cell phone in California while driving."

After flashing an annoyed glance, Jake drove a quarter mile before nabbing a scrap of paper from the after-market cup holder and a pen from the sun visor. "Write down the number and I'll call him when we stop."

Riley did, then folded the map and tucked it away. "Is this the guy we're picking up?"

"No, that's farther up the coast. This is just someone that I need to get ahold of." Hitting the blinker, Jake glanced in the driver's side mirror then changed lanes. "Hungry?"

"Starving."

They'd left without breakfast, so when his dad exited and pulled into a drive-through, Riley accepted the egg burrito and orange juice with a thanks. He bit into the tortilla, thinking of how his mom would freak to know they were eating nothing but fast food. But then again, she probably didn't worry about what her ex-husband did.

Riley glanced at Jake who was focused on the road and wondered why his mom had ever married him in the first place. All he knew of their early days was that his dad had been in Hawaii and Riley's mom—a Californian visiting the Big Island—was at the beach, working on a documentary about environmental economics that never made it to prime time. His dad was waxing his board, awaiting his heat for a tournament.

From what Riley heard, it had been love at first sight because they made a date for that very next day. When wrapping up her afternoon of filming on the shoreline, his mom with her dark hair and slanted brown eyes had been stopped by some talent scout seeing if she'd do a bit of modeling for their swimsuit line.

She skipped the shoot to have fish tacos and a bike ride with Jake Kane.

His mom told him the story once, then never spoke of it again.

Not really wanting to think about his parents' love life, Riley took a swig of orange juice and another bite of burrito. When he finished, he crumpled up his wrapper and tossed it in the back when his dad did. Then there was nothing else to do. Riley stared out the window at the landscape flying by.

There wasn't a lot of beauty to California freeways. Not much more than concrete dividers lining the roadside. A few dry weeds here and there and some litter finished it off. Too many cars. With it a Sunday, most of those cars were probably heading home from weekend travels.

"So who's this friend of yours that we're picking up?" Riley asked.

"Saul?" Jake smiled. "*Mr. Ramirez...*" he added in a really bad Spanish accent. "He's a good man. You'll like him." He ran a hand over his smooth jaw. "Saul's a really tight surfer. Won the ASP twice—"

"How many times have you won it?" Riley interrupted.

"Um..." He ran his hand up and down the side of his face again. "Uh...five times." When Riley was quiet, he continued. "Saul...I met him in Australia when we were teens. Really cool guy. He also does some conservation stuff. A lot like your mom that way. He's sort of an old hippie. Like I said...I think you'll like him."

Riley nodded absently, thinking of how his mom had traded in her hiking boots and nature journal for pom poms and a job that made it possible for her to be with him before and after school every day. "And you guys have a competition in Texas?" He thought of the surfboards strapped to the top of the van. Kind of hard not to with a leash slapping against his window.

But his dad's brow furrowed.

"Isn't Texas where you're headed after you drop me off?"

"Yeah." Jake switched lanes. When he didn't say anything more, Riley figured they'd done their conversation duty for at least the next hour, so he folded his arms over his chest and slouched against the door—remembering that nap he'd wanted to take. He closed his eyes and was nearly asleep when he sensed his dad fidgeting. A few seconds later, the guy was talking to someone.

"Hey. It's Jake."

Riley adjusted his feet but kept his eyes closed, too tired to care who his dad was on the phone with.

"How's the swell up there?" There was a bit of silence, then he said, "Nice. Yeah. I know, it's no North Shore. Dude—I saw your clip, though. That backdoor, man. Whew. *Nice* wave." There was a smile in his voice. "You trying to show me up?"

Another stretch of silence.

"In about a week." He fell quiet a moment. "Yeah, he's here with me."

Not really wanting to do the whole fake sleeping thing, Riley slowly eased himself out of a slouch. He rubbed his eyes with his palms.

"Hey, I'll figure it out. Sponsors'll survive." Jake glanced at Riley, then switched the phone to his other ear and adjusted his one-handed grip on the steering wheel.

Law breaker.

"I'm going to make it work. You just keep me up to date on the water, okay?" His mouth twitched in a smile at whatever the person was saying. "Yeah. I'll see what I can do. Gonna have to work with what I've got."

Riley decided not to try and make sense of that.

"Okay…talk to you later. Bye, man. Travel safe." He hung up and tossed his cell in the dangling cup holder.

They rode without speaking for several miles, each of them taking turns fidgeting.

"Hey, I need to use the bathroom." Riley didn't mean to blurt it out like an eight-year-old, but he was really regretting the bottle of orange juice right now, and with the exits farther and farther apart, he was a bit desperate.

Jake smirked. "You're worse than a toddler."

"You've only got a quarter tank of gas so I'm doing you a favor."

His dad's smirk deepened. "Do you remember the

time that your mom and I drove up to Yosemite and we ended up having to stop for you about every fifteen minutes? It was the longest trip ever."

Riley felt his brow furrow. "When was that?"

His dad wet his lips. "I think it was when we lived in that bungalow in O.C."

Riley hitched his mouth to the side as a gas station came into view. "I was two then. I don't remember anything from when I was two."

The van bumped over the entrance then eased up beside the nearest gas pump. Riley fumbled with the door handle, making a quick escape. He did a beeline for the bathroom, but all he could see in his mind was the picture hanging up in the hallway at his mom's.

He'd walked by it so many times, Riley could still remember her bright grin as the three of them stood at the base of Yosemite's Half Dome, she with her arm looped through Jake's and Riley, just a toddler, sitting atop the man's shoulders. Whoever had taken the photo had stood much too close, because you could make out the chocolate in Riley's hair and clearly see the sparkle in his mom's smiling eyes.

Something about the memory irritated. It wasn't fond, as memories like that should be.

It was empty, maybe muddled. Really…just downright broken. Like thin shells that had been crushed and shattered by waves that were too fierce. Too strong.

Relentless.

Determined to be quick in the gas station, Riley hurried back out to the van. Jake was using the handled scrubber to clean the driver's side of the windshield. With the passenger window freshly polished, Riley looked in the glass and stuck out his tongue to examine his piercing. Because he'd forgotten the little metal barbell, it was healing up. There went sixty bucks and the most painful piercing of his life. Annoyed, he got in and slammed the door too hard. Riley started to slide his headphones back into place.

His dad was settling in. "How about you just turn the music off for a second and enjoy the quiet."

"I don't like the quiet." Riley made himself breathe in through his nose slowly. *Don't get mad.* He let it out and tried to think of something to say that would calm him. But nothing came.

His dad was silent as he turned the ignition. Riley held the headphones in his lap, seriously wanting to put them on—but something deep inside that he could barely find, and barely see all of a sudden—held him back.

The next hour passed in a blur of cars on the bleak freeway, along with three different games on his phone—none of which held his attention because the very thing he needed to be focusing on was a foot away to his left.

Nearly out of distractions, Riley thought about posting a picture to Instagram, but his dad broke the silence.

"We're making good time so we should be to Foster City a little after dark."

"Okay."

"You'll like it. It's a neat place."

He was getting a little tired of hearing what he would like. But Riley drew in a slow breath. His dad was trying here. Maybe time for something more than one-word answers. "How long...how long will it take to get to New Mexico from there?"

"I think a couple of days, but I can map it out better tomorrow." His dad tapped the speedometer that was clicking at him. "How did you meet this family you're helping?"

Unfastening his seatbelt, Riley shifted in the seat then buckled again. "The Fletchers. They live in the town where I do. They're good people."

Jake adjusted his grip on the steering wheel. "I was

really sorry to hear about the accident."

"Yeah. Me too." Riley split open a pack of gum and popped a piece in his mouth. "My friend Becca is really close with her dad." He stuffed the rest into his pocket without offering any over. "I mean…" He whipped the pack out and tried again.

His dad snagged a piece.

"He's not around a lot because he's a truck driver, but they're really close." He had no idea why he said all that about them being close. Especially twice. Maybe conversation was a bad idea.

"Sounds nice."

Riley nodded, then propped the bottoms of his Converse up on the dash, and this time his dad didn't say a word. Riley slipped his earbuds into place and cranked up the volume.

The light in the van dimmed as they passed a semi. A dairy truck by the looks of it. He peered up just as the VW scuttled past the jumbo cab. The bearded driver glanced down and dipped a nod. Riley gave a small one back and thought of Becca's dad—Jay. A man that Riley knew so little about aside from the fact that he faithfully took care of a wife and six kids…and possibly gave his life for a family he didn't even know.

The van slowly left the semi behind, chugging down the freeway barely faster than the eighteen wheelers in the slow lane.

Leaning his head against the rest, Riley glimpsed his reflection in the window. Studied his hair that stuck out in all directions since the only thing he'd been interested in at the crack of dawn was putting on clothes and brushing his teeth. He tugged at the dark locks, wishing he hadn't cut it this way—or maybe wishing he'd just hacked it all…

Most of all he wished that good men didn't have to be in comas. That good children didn't have to watch their dad suffer. Or fear life without him.

Sick of the hyper beat of this song, Riley pulled out the earbuds and rolled them in the cord. He put everything into his backpack. He thought of Becca's letter. Even pulled out the notepad and pen. Maybe there was something he could write to encourage her. But maybe he didn't even know what he was talking about. Riley set the notebook in his lap and kind of wished he could talk to Keith and make sense of all this. Especially since today would have been their day to get together. Riley would have put on the coffee and Keith would come bearing something. Whether a snack, a book, or even a word of wisdom, he never showed up empty handed.

Was it really just three months ago that the man had sat at Riley's kitchen table, laid an enormous, rusty nail on the surface between them, and sipped from his mug like that was the most normal offering in the world? Riley had just looked at him, then to the six inches of pointed steel between them.

"What's that?"

Keith had gestured at him. *"For you."*

Riley had just stared at it, slowly realizing what he meant. His Sunday school teacher had brought a nail like that to show on Easter when he was little. But he hadn't really been paying attention.

Keith spoke. *"That's love and that's grace...and it was for you."*

Riley had shaken his head. Not for him. That was never meant for him. That was for little kids who paid attention in Sunday school and didn't lose all of their friends to fights.

But Keith seemed to believe otherwise. And six weeks ago—after many more discussions over coffee and feather-soft pages of mercy—Riley finally did too.

Still seeing his reflection in the window, Riley stared at himself, catching sight of his dad as well. Riley glanced down to the skull and crossbones on his shirt. Glimpsed the reflection of his mutilated hair. And wondered what— or who—he was really fighting with. It was a Kane, that much was sure. But maybe it wasn't the one in the driver's seat. He shifted, uncomfortable. A few minutes later, he shifted again.

NINE

There were several ways to describe Saul.

Hippie was definitely one of them.

So was *Big Kahuna.* Throw in a dash of *Kurt Russell as Captain Ron* and the man was pretty much nailed down.

They had pulled up in front of the house not two minutes ago. With the dark driveway lit by sconces, Riley stood beside the VW while a guy with a small cross dangling from one ear gave his dad a bear hug—complete with growling. The man stepped back, flip flops slapping against the sidewalk. With a meaty paw, he shoved back a few strands of wild, sun-streaked hair. Wearing a tattered tank and jeans, he looked every bit the over-the-hill surfer Riley had imagined him to be.

This road trip just got so much better.

Regretting having not taken a Greyhound bus, Riley stepped forward when his dad introduced him.

"Aw, brah. This your kid?" The bear of a man closed the gap and shook Riley's hand so hard, Riley's whole arm flopped up and down.

"Hi."

"Dude. He looks just like you." The man slapped Riley on the back.

"Funny how that happens." Jake grinned and motioned toward the house—a funky-looking bungalow with wooden paneling running at odd angles. Even in the dark, the yard seemed as manicured as the rest of the upscale, seaside neighborhood. Riley followed the two men across the lawn, his shoes on the grass a slice of heaven after a day in the car.

"*Mi casa es su casa*," Saul bellowed. He opened the door and they filed into the bright entryway.

Old boards and twisted chunks of driftwood hung from the walls beside modern art that Riley wasn't about to try and make sense of. The leather couch looked pretty decent. Which was good because that was probably where he'd be crashing. The clock on the far wall read 8:15 and the place smelled like coconuts, cigar smoke... and barbecue?

Riley craned his neck to see into the backyard where a grill sat on the porch. Overhead, strands of lights illuminated the night from small palms, softly lighting the yard. Smoke escaped from the closed, stainless steel lid along with a heavenly smell.

"Look atchyou." Jake stepped toward the open French doors and leaned against the jamb to peer out. Shoes already off and in hand, he set them on the back porch.

Riley glanced to Saul who gave him a knowing wink. His dad's bud still wore flip flops, so Riley kept his own shoes on.

"About to throw some steaks on the grill for you boys," the Mexican's voice was husky and weathered, "Corns almost done and I even made my famous slaw. You okay with nuts, kid?"

They both glanced at him and Riley held up a hand. "Just fine."

"K. Cool. Your dad said you might blow up with certain foods."

Riley looked at his dad. "You told him that?"

"I didn't know if he would have stuff around that might make you sick—so yeah, I called him up while you were conked out earlier."

Not sure what to make of that, Riley's brow pinched.

Saul chucked Riley on the shoulder and told him to

head on out.

"Thanks." Riley shoved his hands in his pockets and stepped through the open glass doors and into the quiet night. Voices and music lifted over the fence from a party that was probably a few houses down. It was far enough away that the sound of the waves rose over it.

And that smell...Riley breathed deep of the salty, cool air.

Manning the grill, Saul flipped steaks and Riley watched his dad lean against a post beside him. By the time ten minutes had passed, the two had fallen deep into conversation and his dad was eating from bowls of chips and salsa. Riley wandered around the backyard, happy to stretch his legs.

Pulling out his cell, he saw that he had a text from Becca. It was a picture of her and her little sister, Anna, smiling into the camera with big, goofy grins. Riley grinned right back. He stared at the photo for a couple of minutes, missing Becca in a way that was equal parts sharp and tender. After a while, he turned his camera around and with one of the lit palms beside him, dragged his hand forward through his psycho hair a couple times to style it down, then snapped a picture. He eyed the screen to see if the photo showed up.

It looked pretty decent and his smile had been anything but forced, so he hit send and not a minute later got an adorable text complete with all kinds of hearts and exclamation points. Grinning to himself, Riley scrolled back to her photo. He stood looking at it while his dad flipped the steaks on the grill. Saul brought out plates and silverware. Riley ran his thumb over Becca's heart-shaped face. A swell rose in his chest when he told himself it would just be a couple more days.

Jake called his name then, and Riley glanced over to see them settling down at a wrought iron table. Riley pulled out a chair even as he eyed the feast. A cob of corn sat slathered in melting butter and Saul dipped a pinch of coarse salt then sprinkled it over the top. A scoop of coleslaw was followed by a steak and a hefty dollop of some white sauce.

It looked so good that Riley couldn't even speak. Saul shared a few words of how grateful he was to have the two of them for company, and dipping his head humbly, Jake smiled over at Riley. When Saul started in on his steak, Riley did the same.

After his first bite, he rolled his eyes. "Oh my gosh, this is good."

Saul smiled huge in the dim light. *"Gracias."*

Eyeing the glass of tea beside his plate, Riley sipped. Mint with a dash of a pineapple flavor. "That's amazing."

"Saul's a chef," Jake said. "When he wants to be."

Saul chuckled. Riley smiled at the exchange and dunked a forkful of steak into what he now knew as blue cheese sauce. His dad and Saul continued their catch-up which kept his focus out of the conversation and on eating. He was good with that because after a few more bites, he wished he could just up and take a bath in the slaw. With nuts and dried cranberries and some kind of sweet and tangy sauce, it was the best thing he'd ever eaten.

Later, while his dad and Saul swapped stories, Riley lay in a hammock, looking up at the clear night sky. The party had died down so with the sound of waves easier to hear now, he knew the ocean was only a few steps past the back gate. Stars glittered overhead. He pointed to one, then the other, squinting in search of something he might recognize. He'd checked the time a few minutes ago and it was just after ten. Riley used a foot to gently nudge the hammock from side to side—letting the day wash out of him.

Not that it was a bad day.

He didn't even know how to describe it.

Maybe that's why he was so tired. He'd added to Becca's letter during the last hour on the road. An entire page more and he felt a strange sense of lightness. Like he had all these pieces to him that he needed to try and make sense of. Pieces that he'd been ignoring and cramming out of sight for far too long. He rubbed his fingertips over his forehead and shifted to peer over to where Jake and Saul sat laughing around the table. The strung lights glinted off the glasses they drank from and never had Riley seen two men look more like best buds.

Peering back up at the sky, Riley braced his foot against the ground as he kept the hammock swaying. Beyond tired, he closed his eyes but didn't let himself lay that way for too long or he'd fall asleep.

He rose from the creaking hammock and told his dad he was ready to crash.

"Guest room's yours if you want it," Jake said.

"No. I'm fine. You take it. I'm good with the couch."

Saul said he'd laid out some blankets and Riley thanked him. In the house he saw that Saul had added a few plush pillows—so tempting he could collapse right then and there.

But probably a good idea to brush his teeth first. Riley grabbed his clear Ziploc bag and ventured down the hall until he found a bathroom. He dug through the bag and pulled out his shaving stuff and EpiPen in search of toothpaste. While he brushed, Riley eyed the long tube that was his prescription. When he was little, his mom always got three at a time: one for the house, one for her purse, and one for Riley to wear around his waist at school in a horrible little Velcro thing which he'd long-since ditched. Since he only used them if he had an allergic reaction to something, he rarely gave the epinephrine shots much thought. Which had him picking this one up and turning it over to check the date. He squinted at the numbers. Six months expired.

Riley rinsed his mouth and turned the faucet off.

His last allergic reaction had been a couple of years ago, so he was getting better at being careful with what he ate. Still, he turned the vial of medicine in his fingers and gave it a light shake. He was pretty sure the shots worked okay even after the expiration date. At least that's what he had read. Or maybe his mom had told him that. Likely he'd seen it on some Facebook post and that person didn't know what they were talking about and now he was going to die.

"Awesome." Riley stashed the prescription away. "Nothing like the warm fuzzies before bed."

He heard the back door open, followed by voices. Beyond tired, Riley zipped up the bag and decided it was time to figure out if that couch was as comfortable as it looked.

"Hey. Earth to Riley."

At someone shaking his shoulder, Riley opened his eyes.

His dad peered down at him, then sipped from a mug. "I thought you were dead for a second." He smiled—his face smooth. Whether from genes or a fresh shave, Riley didn't know.

Riley ran his hand over his eyes and the leather couch creaked as he sat up.

"You certainly slept the sleep of the dead."

No kidding. "What time is it?"

"About ten."

"Oh gosh… sorry."

"Don't worry. We're in no hurry today." Wearing shorts and flip flops, Jake was bare from the waist up. Dried salt water dusted the tops of his brown shoulders. "Saul and I gotta take care of some stuff and we'll hit the road tomorrow. That still okay?"

Riley rubbed at his eyes, remembering that was the plan. "Yeah, that's fine."

Bumming around Saul's wasn't exactly how he hoped to spend this day. Not when he should already be in New Mexico. But at least they were well fed.

Riley said that last bit out loud. Jake chuckled and told him that there was a mean quiche on the kitchen counter. Ten minutes later, Riley was digging into his second slice. Then, while his dad and Saul went out to the garage to do whatever they needed to do, Riley carried some clean clothes into the bathroom and changed. He threw on a hat, grabbed the skateboard from the top rack of the VW, and hit the sidewalk.

His dad called after him that there would be a lot of people about and to "Stay off the radar."

With a thumbs up, Riley pulled his hat lower.

Riley knew that most people didn't recognize him off the amateur circuit. But when he started to get invites from sponsors and his name landed in skate magazines...people started to look at him differently. There was a reason he lived in the middle of nowhere.

His dad playing it cool the other night had been a bunch of baloney. There was no way Jake didn't know that his very own sponsor had called his son six months ago offering him the moon and the stars if he'd sign with them.

Riley hadn't been able to hang up on them fast enough.

The beach neighborhood was mellow and the weather perfect. Seeing a park across the street, he rode in that direction. The moist air clung to his skin and made his t-shirt heavy and cool. Seagulls darted overhead. A pair of girls ambled by on shiny beach cruisers. He ollied over the curb, then sped across the quiet intersection to a park. Balloons bobbed beside a birthday party. It must have been a school holiday or something. A young guy and girl were flying a kite, looking so in love that Riley smiled.

Peeling his gaze away from them, he tried not to think about Becca being so far. He held onto his dad's promise that they would head back down south in the morning. It couldn't come soon enough.

But since he had a day to burn, he started toward the parking lot where a rise of stairs had gathered skaters like moths to a flame. Riley skidded to a stop there, and several people glanced his way. Hitching board to hand, Riley gave a muted smile. He eyed the main attraction that a few of the bravest guys were attempting—two sets of eight stairs with a concrete landing in between. Tough.

A twenty-something with dreads had everyone cheering when he boardslid the top handrail, and a couple of punks with bad skills and attitudes to match were ogling the posse of teenage girls who had camera phones poised—taking selfies, likely.

Hat still low, Riley skated around doing tailslides on a cement block, keeping to himself—as he'd promised.

It took twenty minutes for him to blow his cover. Which was almost a record. It wasn't until he got bored and decided to launch himself off the top flight of stairs in a kickflip that anyone looked his way. He sailed past all eight steps, touched down on the center landing, then ollied up to boardslide the bottom handrail. Wood grated against metal and he landed in a smooth carve to the left. Finished, he did a grind on the nearest parking block to celebrate having not just killed himself.

That's when he heard his name. And his dad's.

TEN

It was actually one of the girls who'd spoken. She had big, curly hair, a round face, and enormous eyes. *Modeling-type* was written all over her and her cut-off shorts. Riley started up the stairs with his head bowed.

He rode back to the cement block but wasn't in the mood for tail grinds anymore. Maybe he should just find a storm drain to skate in—or better yet, go join that birthday party—because the girl who'd outed him kept looking his way. Her crew of chicks was doing more hair-flipping, leg-crossing, and giggling. And now some of the guys were asking questions—what it was like to be him, if he'd decided who he was going to sign with yet, and if he'd learned his moves from his dad. One guy even asked him to sign his board. The other half were just glaring. Riley answered them all best he could, saving the hardest answer for last.

"Yeah—I learned a few things from my dad." Which wasn't a total lie.

The guy owed him.

He had to catch his breath. Riley sat a few feet away on the block and placed his board beside him. Overhead, the sky was a bright blue and a breeze cooled him down.

He had no doubt that every skater here dreamed of being sponsored. Different brands offered free clothes, shoes, boards, parties. You name it. And if Riley rode as well as they thought? Some seriously nice paychecks. Which would send him from sponsored to pro.

But he didn't want to be a professional anything. He just wanted to have a regular job, eat meatloaf every Friday night, and watch his *someday* kids play little league.

He bent to fix the lace on his shoe and was just straightening the bottom of his jeans when he realized the curly-haired girl was walking over. She held up a glittery purple phone that matched her nails and asked if she could take a picture with him.

"Um…" Riley straightened his shirt, tugging at it in an attempt to cool down some more. "I'm not really the picture type."

She tipped her head to the side as if he'd just said she was the cutest thing since baby bunnies. "Just *one*?" Her sculpted brows rose and she waggled her phone at him.

"Honestly. Sorry. I just don't take pictures." Next would come the pout.

Which she nailed.

He kept his gaze on the safe spots—her face, her feet. Getting from one to the other was nothing but trouble so he did it as fast as humanly possible. Her eyes were even bigger and brighter up close.

She asked how long he was in town and what he was doing later.

Riley swallowed hard. He had absolutely nothing to offer her. He hoped she'd know that. "I kinda have a girlfriend."

"What side of *kinda*?" She bit a glossy pink lip.

"The serious side."

She let out a breath, and not wanting to be a complete jerk, Riley rose and grabbed his board before reaching out to shake her hand. She seemed surprised as he released her fingers, so he used the opportunity to make his escape.

He shot a subtle wave and skated back across the park before that got any messier.

He meant to ride straight back, but glanced over to the middle of the parking lot where a couple of kids were struggling with kick flips. One of the first skateboard tricks to learn. A little squirt was doing it all wrong, so Riley pulled up and offered pointers.

The kid gave it a few more tries. Riley turned his hat around backwards and knelt to angle the little one's front foot on a diagonal. He told him to kick across the deck harder. The other youngsters joined in and their enthusiasm was contagious. Next thing he knew, he had showed all of them, a half hour had passed, and they were nearly landing the trick.

Realizing he needed to get back, Riley gave them all high-fives. He tugged his hat off and crammed the soft side into his back pocket. His foot pumped against the asphalt, sending him flying toward Saul's. And nearly into an elderly woman in a wheelchair. Grumbling, she shook her finger at him. Then at his board. Then his hair. Riley apologized for everything.

A few minutes later, he'd loaded her picnic basket and blanket into her trunk and she was pinching his cheek.

As he rode across the street to Saul's, Riley spotted a yard sale on the corner closest to the park. Saul was there in the driveway, poking through a box of stuff. The seaside wind was picking up. Riley stepped off the skateboard and carried it up the steep driveway. "Where's my dad?"

Without speaking, Saul thumbed over his shoulder toward his house. Then he straightened and held out two CD cases for Riley to see. *"My Side of the Mountain* or *Black Beauty?"*

"Are you being serious?"

"Dead serious, *mijo*. They're books on tape. Or CD, I guess. Passes the time on the road."

Riley just stared at him.

"Pick, or I'll do it. And I guarantee it'll be *Black Beauty."*

"Uh…" He eyed the two cover images, then pointed to the one on the left that looked less painful. "The boy with the falcon."

"My Side of the Mountain it is. Pretty sure I read this once."

Riley was just glad he had his iPod.

Saul paid three dollars for the audio book and a plaid golf hat which he wore backwards as he waited for Riley to fish fifty cents from his pocket for a couple of bent nails that were stuck together. One of those puzzles that's supposedly easy to solve, yet no one can ever figure them out. At the very least it would give him something to do in the car.

Back at his house, Saul tapped a button and the

garage door groaned open.

Riley spotted his dad. Leaning over an old table covered in splayed-out maps. Not this again.

"Getting anywhere?" Saul asked as they entered the dim garage.

Jake looked up from what he was doing. "Sort of." At his elbow sat an open laptop that looked like it was logged into the Weather Channel. "Where were you two?"

"Well, while your offspring was getting *fangirled* at the park, I was at a yard sale." The scraggly-haired Mexican motioned the way they'd come.

"So not true," Riley said.

"I do think I can see across the street. And you were definitely getting fangirled. *Twice*."

Knee up, Riley blocked the playful jab Saul chucked his way, then apologized to his dad for not staying off the radar so well.

Jake just waved it off, but he did glance up the street.

"I almost bought a set of clubs, but I don't use the ones I have." Saul adjusted his backwards hat. "And your kid wants to listen to *My Side of the Mountain* in the car."

Riley fiddled with one of the studs in his ears as he walked past, then returned a good-natured punch to Saul's hard arm.

By the time he stashed the board, his dad and Saul were debating whether or not they should give the van an oil change. Judging by the sound of the engine, Riley voted for change and even offered to do it. No complaints to that. Saul brought him the oil pan and Riley slid it in place then pulled the plug. His dad and Saul had their heads together—two surf bums talking about swells and other stuff that made no sense. He glimpsed the top map. Maybe he'd gotten a D in geography, but the spattering of Hawaiian islands was definitely not Texas.

"When do you think we'll be leaving?" Riley asked.

His dad exchanged a glance with Saul. "We could probably be out of here by breakfast tomorrow. Noon at the latest."

Not wanting to be in their way, and since the oil would take a little while to drain, Riley went inside. He grabbed a soda from the fridge and sank into the couch to check in with his mom.

Phone in hand, he tapped the email icon first and saw that he had a dozen new messages there. He scrolled through them, noticing the monthly newsletter from Harmony Farms. Mrs. Lawrence sent them out and chicks totally dug them. A recipe, a coupon for a dollar off of birdseed, and a few pictures from around the store. This edition featured Riley and Mr. Lawrence playing chess by the wood stove on a slow day.

Awesome. The gig was up; he had no life.

Riley smiled, remembering the way his boss had creamed him. Right after he'd mentioned again that if Riley wanted to take over the store in the next few years, to just say the word.

That was followed by *checkmate* and Mrs. Lawrence bringing over oatmeal cookies.

Missing home, Riley pulled up his mom's number. He was about to dial it, but maybe it would be nicer to see her. He deleted the digits, switched over to FaceTime, and waited while it connected.

Her smiling face appeared on the screen a second later. "Riles! To what do I owe this pleasure?"

"Hi Mom." He grinned. "How's it going?"

"It's going good."

"How's the tournament?" He popped the metal top on the can.

"Great. The girls placed second and now we're heading home." She always took the less-is-more approach these days when discussing her squad, which was good.

When she shifted her phone to the other hand, Riley

made out the shapes and colors of a hotel room in the background.

"How are things going with you and your dad?"

"Fine." Riley swigged the cold soda.

"*Okay…*" she said slowly. "Now how about the long answer—how are things going with you and your dad?"

Riley smirked. "It's pretty good. It's not so bad, I guess. Kind of slow going. We're at his buddy's house, somewhere up the coast. I can't remember the name of the town, but it took about a day to get here."

"Does that buddy happen to be named Saul?"

"About six foot five? Looks like a cross between a bear and a pirate?"

She smiled with those straight white teeth of hers. "That's the one."

All kids probably thought their mom was pretty, but his had something special about her that he'd never quite been able to pin down and, frankly, had never tried. A mixture of American and several Pacific Island heritages made her face exotic. A little Japanese gave a shape to her eyes and face that was so striking—to his annoyance—men were always looking her way.

That face was still smiling across the screen from him. "And…"

"Uh…" He also hated the way she always wanted details that actually mattered. "And I guess it's pretty good. Saul feeds us well, but he and dad have some stuff with maps and the Weather Channel to figure out so…" He shrugged.

She squinted a little, as if trying to make sense of that. Made two of them.

Except there was something in her expression that had Riley wondering what she knew that he didn't. He was about to ask, but she spoke first.

"How are the Fletchers? How is Jay?"

"Becca's dad is doing okay, I think." Riley set the soda on the coffee table. "She said he's still in the coma but is stable, so I think that's a good sign."

Saul stepped into the living room just as his mom agreed that it was. Saul held up a quart of oil then two fingers and mouthed the words that he was heading to the store.

Riley gave him a thumbs up.

"Sometimes, even, doctors induce a coma to allow a patient to—" His mom's voice clipped to an end and her eyes widened.

Certain he was being attacked by a sea monster, Riley glanced over his shoulder. Hands in pockets, his dad just stared at the phone. Riley didn't know what to say, but it didn't really matter because his dad stepped around the couch and eased himself to a sit.

His mom was still quiet.

"Hey, Jess."

"Jake."

Riley's heart pounded. His dad glanced to him, then back at the screen. Riley realized that while his mom probably saw his dad through magazines or websites, his dad hadn't seen his mom in years. When the staring between the two got downright awkward, Riley shoved the phone into Jake's hand and lied about needing to use the bathroom. Saul poked around in a rolltop desk and patted his back pocket as if looking for his wallet.

At the edge of the hall, Riley glanced back just as his dad began talking in low tones. Riley wanted to smile, but checked it as he left the room. No sense in still hoping for something that would never be.

In the bathroom, he went through the motions of brushing his teeth and washing his hands just to stall. Hands still dripping, he rested them on the edge of the sink and looked at his reflection in the mirror. Having not shaved in a couple days, now was as good a time as any. And his bag of toiletries was still on the counter. He wet his face and squirted shaving cream into his palm, then wondered what his mom and dad were talking about. If they were even still talking. Curious, he made quick work of shaving and stashed his stuff in the jumbo, clear bag.

Back down the hall, he heard his dad talking sharper than before. He said something about Hawaii when Riley stepped into the room.

Jake's back was to him. "I *know* it's January." He gripped a shoulder that was folded, bowed. "*Hawaii*...I know about that too." He pronounced it Ha-*wah*-ii. Just as Riley always remembered. Except right now the word came out dry. Almost condescending to whoever had asked him that.

Keys in hand, Saul leaned against the opposite doorway, expression hard.

Riley's phone sat on the coffee table with a dark screen. So his mom was gone.

"Yeah...I know that, as well. Look... I said I'd do my best and that's all I can do at this point." He went quiet, listening to whatever the other person said. "I already talked to the guy and I'm going to compensate him out of pocket." Propping an elbow up against the wall beside the sliding glass door, Jake gripped the back of his head, nodding in rhythm with the voice clicking over on the line. "Yes, I know how much that's gonna cost."

For a second, Riley wondered if this had to do with his dad's request for him to not blow his cover. But he was pretty sure it didn't. He moved to sit on the couch so that he'd be seen in case this wasn't a conversation he was supposed to hear. The moment his dad spotted him, his shoulders relaxed, head tilting to the floor.

"And no, I can't bring him with me. You're just not getting the situation and it's not really something that I'm going to explain to you." Still holding the cell to his ear, he nodded at what the caller responded with.

Riley waited—trying to ignore the sudden tide of emotions inside him.

"Yeah, I'll stop and pick them up tomorrow. I'll overnight everything to you." Jake listened, dipped his head in a single nod, then with a punch of his thumb, ended the call.

"Sponsors?" Saul asked from his same spot.

Jake hesitated. "And then some." He glanced around the room—looking not nearly as famous as Riley always imagined him. He seemed tired. Almost scared. Finally, he released a determined sigh. "Let's hit the road."

"Like...*now*?" Riley watched him cross the room toward the garage.

"I want to be out of here within the hour."

Riley and Saul exchanged a look. His dad disappeared into the garage and slammed the door behind him.

ELEVEN

"Did you really start smoking that young?" Becca had asked.

"I did, I'm sorry to say."

"And you don't smoke anymore?"

"No."

"What made you stop?"

"My mom told me that if I smoked one more cigarette, she'd take away my car. Then I told her that if she smoked one more, I'd crash *hers."*

Becca's eyes had gone wide. *"What happened?"*

"She grounded me for talking back to her. Then a week later, we signed up for some class. Neither of us have smoked since and we both have pins that say 'smoke free and happy.'"

Becca smiled. *"I'm proud of you. Both of you."*

"Thanks. I like my car. And my lungs. And my mom."

She laughed. The sound perfect—

The VW jerked. Half asleep, Riley opened his eyes, memories falling away.

Lying on the center seat of the van, he slowly sat up. Saul was in the passenger's seat, a cigarette between two fingers where his hand rested on the window ledge. He pocketed a lighter with the other. Riley's mouth was watering. He wiped his nose from the smell and his dad glanced behind him.

"Hey." He hit Saul's arm then tossed his head in Riley's direction. "Kid just quit. Put it out, will ya?"

Of *all* the things for his mom to fill him in on…

"Oh. Yeah. Sorry." Saul tapped the cigarette out in a paper cup, then glanced back at Riley with an apologetic smile.

"No problem, man. I don't mind." But his senses were going nuts so Riley pushed on the window until it inched open.

"I thought you'd quit too, come to think of it," his dad said to Saul.

Saul shrugged. "You stress me out, I think."

Jake smirked and shook his head.

Riley rubbed at the mess that was his hair. Late morning light streamed in through the window. "What time is it? Where are we?"

"'Bout ten," Saul said, looking like he'd been sleeping too. Thanks to the oil change, it had been nearly nightfall by the time they got the van set to rights and Saul had convinced Jake that they should just set off in the morning. A couple hours ago to be exact. "Your dad may be ready to switch drivers. Someone here didn't get much sleep, I think And we could use fuel."

"I'll drive for a while," Riley offered. He needed some stimulation.

A few minutes later his dad pulled the Volkswagen into a station and parked beside a pump. Riley slid his card into the machine, and while his dad set the nozzle into place, followed Saul across to a coffee shop. By the time they walked back out, he held a mocha just so he could shovel whipped cream into his mouth with the straw. A second, he gave to his dad.

Riley took the driver's seat, buckled in, and nearly scalded his tongue on the first sip of coffee. After a few seconds of figuring out where everything was on the vintage van, Riley pushed the clutch, put the beast in first, and pulled back out.

Ahead? New Mexico.

He thought back to his dream. Well, more of a memory because he'd been sitting beside Becca in her trailer while she asked one of her many questions about his life and who he was. As if she was trying to figure him out before giving him her heart. He always answered her honestly because he'd been quickly losing his own.

Spotting a side street that could lead him over to the I-5, Riley quick-glanced over his shoulder for an opening in traffic so he could get in the left lane. The seaside road with its stop lights and pedestrians was already making him claustrophobic.

"What are you doing?" Saul asked.

"Taking the 5 freeway." Checking his side mirror again, Riley changed lanes.

"No. Stay on the PCH," Jake said sleepily.

"It's going to be so much slower," Riley countered.

They passed another turnout for a surfing spot. Bike riders ambled by and a minivan was practically in his lane with its blinker on while it waited for a parking spot. The two-lane Pacific Coast Highway was a nightmare.

"We need to take it." Arms folded, his dad leaned against the window.

With yet another side street sailing by, Riley eased back on the gas pedal. "Why?"

"*Es mas bonita.*" Saul kissed closed fingertips toward the ocean on his right.

But Riley knew this was about a lot more than seaside views. "Dad?"

"Just stay on the PCH or I'll drive."

Blowing out a breath, Riley tightened his grip on the steering wheel and veered back into the right lane to keep from exiting the highway that wound along the coast from Washington to Mexico. A light up ahead turned from yellow to red and he slowed to a stop behind a silver sports car. Riley sat all but fuming until the light turned green. The stupid VW chugged down the road.

"This is ridiculous," he muttered under his breath when he had to slow for another light. "This has to do with surfing, doesn't it?"

Jake spoke, sounding half asleep. "It's not about anything that you need to worry about."

"Fine, I'll just pull over and we can talk on the side of the road." Glancing in the rearview, Riley slammed the blinker on.

Those nearly-black eyes opened. "How about we just skip New Mexico altogether and I drop you back off at your Jeep?"

Riley tapped the blinker so it shut off. He felt Saul glance at him, then look back over his shoulder. A subtle shake of his head and Saul gave the jerk a disapproving look.

Riley glanced in the rearview again as his dad sunk lower on the bench seat and pulled up the hood of his sweatshirt. He leaned his head against the window and closed his eyes. Riley hoped he'd sprain his neck sitting that way.

Ten miles down the road, the guy was out.

"What's this all about?" Riley asked Saul quietly.

"You mean aside from being bad with humans?" Saul bent and snatched up the thick, plastic CD case from the yard sale. "He's upset."

"About...?"

Saul studied the cracked cover of the audio book before snapping it open. "It's a long story and I think it's better if he tells you himself, *mijo*." He ejected whatever was in the player, swapped the discs, and turned the volume lower before hitting play. The narrator started in a strong, clear voice, introducing the story, author, and copyright. Saul nudged the volume down a smidge more. "Mind if we listen to this for a while? Maybe it will keep the peace." He flashed a muted smile.

Riley shrugged a shoulder. "Fine with me."

The story began with the narrator talking about a snowstorm, and how he, as a boy, was holed up in a mountain, living in a tree after having run away from home…and his dad. Too frustrated to listen, Riley tuned it out. But Saul looked focused on whatever the narrator was going on about. The shaggy-haired Mexican had an elbow on the window ledge and was tugging at his goatee, gaze glued to the dashboard. The story.

Loosening his grip on the steering wheel, Riley leaned back against his seat. Now would be a good time to count to ten. Pretty much the cheesiest thing, though, and it only worked sometimes. Maybe better to think of three things he was happy about. Riley had tried it a few times and it actually worked.

Of course he didn't remember to do it as often as he should, but the thought came to mind as the highway curved toward the sea, overlooking glittering water and waves, more stop lights ahead.

One—at least they were headed south. That was a big positive. Two—he was in a vehicle that actually worked. Another positive. Sure it was annoying that it couldn't go over fifty without catapulting them out of their seats—

Good things, Riley.

He settled deeper into the driver's seat. Okay, he could do this.

Three...

Riley glanced in the rearview mirror to where his dad was asleep. Three...

Jake adjusted his position and didn't seem all that asleep anymore.

Riley shot out a sigh. He had nothing for three. But he made himself think on it until he did. Finally, he decided that the third positive could be the fact that they were listening to a story about a kid who lived like a wild boy, *as opposed* to a book about a horse named Beauty. Definite perk. So maybe this three things business wasn't all that hard. If he had to do it again in another ten miles, well, so be it.

Turns out he kind of had to. Traffic on the PCH was that slow.

By noon, Riley had a whole list of things he was thankful for—so the hours weren't a total bust. Never once did the ocean leave their right-hand side. Though it was blocked by buildings as they passed through the different towns, there was often a straight-shot view of the water and waves. It was…sort of pretty.

But that's not what made his list.

It was in the little things he spotted. A couple of guys cliff diving—laughing and flinging themselves off a rocky ledge into the foamy water below. A pair of teens walking along one of the paths carrying a turned-over canoe. A chalkboard sign outside of a coffee shop saying *'Our Wi-Fi is broken. Have a conversation.'*

People salsa dancing at one of the little cafes.

Life.

The salsa dancing would have turned his mom's head. So would the canoe. And probably the cliff diving. She was adventurous like that. She was the one who had taken him to fly kites and on hikes all over Southern California. She was also the one who had driven him nearly every day to the skate park so he could fling himself off of ramps and rails.

It was probably that side of her that landed her on a date with one of the most prestigious surfers in the world. The embodiment of heroic.

Well, in the water at least. Not so much in other ways. Something Riley—and his mom—had learned the hard way.

Because when you're twelve and you read your

mom's diary, some things come across loud and clear. Riley shifted, wishing he hadn't thought of that right now. Wishing once again that he didn't know that the famous athlete had suggested his girlfriend have it *taken care of*— right after she told him he would be a dad. Maybe Riley would never know what else was said or how hard his dad had pushed, but tear-stained pages say enough.

Something flashed in his side vision and Riley glanced past his shoulder to see that his cell, in the mesh pouch of his backpack, was lit up with a call. And since his dad was using that backpack for a pillow, the vibration's buzzing had to be in his ear.

Jake swatted in his sleep.

Another buzz, another swat. Jake grumbled something, then swatted again.

In the passenger's seat, Saul turned away from his word search and used the little book to whack him in the leg. "Hey, wake up!"

Jake jolted upright.

"You're just dreaming. It's my phone," Riley blurted, trying to shake off all thoughts of his dad and his mom and what he wished he'd never snuck into her closet and read.

The call stopped. Jake leaned forward, head nearly

even with the front seats, and rubbed his eyes with the heels of his palms. "How long was I out?"

"A couple of hours." Slipping the pen behind his ear, Saul went back to his puzzle.

Riley tipped his head toward his shoulder. "Say, hand me my cell, will you?"

After a shuffle and the sound of a zipper, Jake held forward the phone. "It's illegal to talk on your phone while driving."

Ignoring that well-played remark, Riley glanced at the screen and saw that the missed call was the auto shop where he'd left his Jeep.

"I'm pretty sure that's why they invented speaker phones—ooh!" Saul sat up straighter and used the dash as a table while he circled a word. A thick, silver ring around his thumb caught the sunlight. "Def-en-es-tration." His brow dug in. "What on earth does that mean?" He skimmed to the bottom of the page then announced that it was the act of throwing someone out a window. He glanced to Riley. "I promise not to *defenestration* you at any point during this trip. As to your dad, I make no guarantees."

A chuckle came from the backseat.

One-handing the wheel, Riley grinned as he tapped

the redial button for the mechanic. He set his phone on his thigh and waited for it to ring. Hopefully they'd be able to hear him okay. Especially with the loudest engine in the universe in the back of this bus.

A man's voice broke through. "Pierce Auto Shop."

"Hi. This is Riley Kane and I dropped my Jeep off there a couple days ago. I just got a call from you guys."

"Oh, yeah. We've got your estimate for the new transmission on the Jeep."

Riley swallowed, wishing this wasn't about to be broadcast to the whole car. "'K. What is it?"

The mechanic stated a sum that was a couple lift tickets over a grand.

Riley stretched his neck from side to side. "Okay. Thanks." It was a fair price for a transmission overhaul. About what he'd expected. Still…he was going to have to stack a lot of hay bales to make it. After squaring away the details with the mechanic, Riley ended the call. He reached back and dropped his cell into the open backpack behind him. He sat without speaking. Saul and his dad were silent too.

"Um…" Leaning forward, Jake dipped his head and spoke softly. "If you need help with that—"

Riley shook his head. "I don't."

His dad settled against his seat again. "You sure?"

Keeping his eyes on the road, Riley tipped his head toward the back. "Positive." A few months of work should square him away with enough funds. It was going to be okay.

Jake sat quiet. Saul glanced between the two of them, then uncapped his pen.

Folding a leg up on the opposite knee, Saul's flip flop bounced as he searched. "Okay, here's another one. *Aquiver*. Sounds like something JELL-O does."

Riley squinted, trying to mentally shift from transmissions to JELL-O.

"It says you get extra points if you can use it in a sentence. How about…the ladies go all *aquiver* when Saul walks by?"

Riley smirked. "Good one."

Chin to chest, Saul searched for another. "All right. Your turn, *mijo*." He capped his pen. "Ineffable."

"What kind of word search is this?" Riley spared a glance.

"Just use it in a sentence. It means 'too great to be expressed in words.'"

"Easy." One hand still on the wheel, Riley plucked at the collar of his t-shirt. "My good looks are *ineffable*."

"Dang. I wish I got that word."

Riley chuckled.

"Okay, we gotta give one to your dad." Saul crossed the word out, then took a second before circling another. "All right. Big Kane!"

"I'm not doing it." Plastic crackled as Jake tore into a bag of chips.

Saul motioned to him with his pen. "You have to. We did it."

"That's the stupidest game ever."

"No, it's not. It's fun. Play. I'll give you a dollar."

"A *dollar*?"

"Yeah, which is like an iced tea at the next gas station. Okay. Your word is…hiraeth."

"Hear-a-who?"

Saul repeated the word, then searched for the definition. He squinted at the fine print beneath the puzzle. "It means a homesickness for a home you can't return to…or that never was."

Riley wet his lips. Saul fell quiet. That picture from Yosemite flashed through Riley's mind. And a million other moments that never were.

Maybe this was a bad idea.

The van just hummed down the highway.

But Jake sighed, leaned forward, and wagged a finger in thought as if unfazed. "All right. I'll play." He smoothed a hand over his mouth, then snapped his fingers. "Being inside this van makes me...what's the word?"

Saul repeated it.

"Being inside this van makes me heer-ay-eth for a convertible."

Riley snorted, worry falling away.

"Pronunciation fail!" Saul bellowed. "But good effort on the sentence. What do you think?" He glanced at Riley. "I'd say like a 4.0 *maybe* 4.5."

"You think that high?"

"Dude, you guys are ruthless!" Jake tapped his shoe against Saul's seat and crunched a chip.

"Should we give him his dollar?" Riley asked, knowing that his dad had been smart to bring Saul along. Because the man with the big smile and loud laugh had a way of softening this day...this trip. One more thing to be thankful for. Maybe his dad knew what he was doing after all. At least a little bit.

"Yeah, we'll give him his dollar." Riley glanced in the rearview mirror to see that his dad was peering out the window and smiling.

When he glanced Riley's way though, the smile faded some and Riley wondered if they both had an alternate definition for that word of his.

Jake cleared his throat. "There's a ride shop in about two miles." He stated the name of his biggest sponsor. "You won't be able to miss it. I just need to stop in for a second."

Riley nodded.

"You do see what you're wearing?" Saul spoke without looking up from his puzzle.

Jake muttered something, and Riley glanced over his shoulder just as his dad whipped off his shirt. With a click, his seatbelt fell free. He threw the shirt on the seat, crawled to his knees, and dug in the back.

Saul pointed to a bright blue shop on the right. Racks of boards and wetsuits flanked the open doors. Riley was pretty sure that was his dad, third from the left in a huge wall mural of famous surfers. He pulled the van into a parking spot. Jake twisted back around, tugging a shirt down over his abdomen with the same logo as the sign overhead. And Saul's hat.

An elite brand of clothing and gear that represented a chain renowned the world over—one of the very companies that made their free and lavish lifestyle possible.

The Hawaiian slipped on sunglasses and opened his door. "Keep the engine on."

Riley put the van in neutral and pulled the parking break. "Gonna rip off the place?"

Those smile lines appeared. "Very funny." He climbed out and hustled past oblivious customers and into the shop.

When Saul offered to drive, Riley unbuckled his seatbelt and reached for the handle of the door. "Think this place has a bathroom?"

"No, no, no, no," Saul blurted. He thumbed a path for Riley to crawl to the back, and when Riley did, Saul switched seats by sliding over.

Riley was about to complain that he really had to go but didn't want to sound like a baby...and his dad was already stepping out of the store's doorway, a big box in his grip.

"Unless you want to get hung up," Saul added distractedly as he watched. "Cool guys working here, but if we go in, it'll be a few hours and a couple of Instagram posts before we get out. Especially with you in tow." Saul smiled over at him. "Some PR of your dad and his Mini-Me is just what they'd like to see. The first ever picture of the two of you together? Golden."

Which was exactly what Riley didn't want.

Squinting toward the shop, he watched a few people peer toward the van as his dad walked to it. Jake whipped open one of the side doors, crammed in the box that was heavy enough to send a jolt through the floorboard, then slammed the door. He flashed his confused-looking friends a peace sign and slid in the passenger's seat. Saul tipped the bill of his hat in their direction then threw the gears into reverse. Jake barely closed his door and the van was backing out.

So much for using the bathroom.

"Success?" Saul asked the man beside him.

"Like a pro."

TWELVE

The audiobook narrator talked about the first fire the boy in the story had ever lit. How it was magic and how in the dead of winter, something so simple as sticks and grass created a warm light that cracked and snapped...filling the woods with brightness. Warming the trees. Making them more friendly. Holding back the night.

As Riley listened, he realized that the van had been mostly silent for the last several hours since their lunch stop. Saul drove with a goofy expression as if this were his favorite book in the whole world. Riley hated to admit it, but he was in his own kind of trance.

Sitting in the back, shoes propped up on his duffle bag so his feet wouldn't fall asleep again, Riley shook his head to keep himself alert. Because he never gelled it, the front of his mohawk flopped onto his forehead. He shoved it away.

"There's a good spot coming up in about twenty miles," Saul said.

Perfect. Their last stop hadn't been much of anything.

At least they'd found him a gas station.

Saul shifted in the driver's seat. "We can grab dinner, stretch our legs, and if everyone's up for it, find a hotel for the night."

"Sold." Riley pulled at the side of his hair to see if it was growing.

From the front, Jake chimed in about being able to one-up a hotel, and within a few seconds, they all agreed to the beach house he had access to. Not nearly as interested in complaining about the PCH as he'd been that morning, Riley realized that his dad probably had connections all the way south. He thought of the map in the glove compartment, all those numbers.

"This story makes me want to live in the woods," Saul said out of the blue.

Since watching his hair grow meant an all-time low, Riley grabbed the CD case from the floor and eyed the cover—a scene of a boy of about ten or so, all alone in the wilderness. The back text described how he had run away from home. Something about having a different dream than his dad's. "Gonna live in a hollowed-out tree, too?"

"Heck yeah. That's the best part. And I wanna wear

deer skins and get a falcon like this kid had. Could you imagine having a bird like that?"

Riley smiled at the guy's enthusiasm. "That *would* be pretty cool. I don't think I'd want to climb that cliff, though, to get it."

"But that's the beauty of it. Kid runs away from home and finds himself all alone in the wild. Didn't have anything but a knife—"

"A *pen* knife," Riley corrected.

"*Exactamente*. He barely had a thing, but he knew what he needed to survive. He could have risked his neck for food or shelter, or even getting back home…but he did it for a baby bird. I think he knew that if he could climb up to the nest, get a falcon, and raise it up as his own, he'd have a buddy. And a crazy-cool form of survival. That bird was everything to him."

Jake cleared his throat. "Speaking of survival…are we almost there? 'Cause when you two pansies are done with your book club, I wanna get some grub."

Riley chuckled and Saul joined in. Soon, his dad was laughing too.

Jake hitched his phone out of his back pocket and leaned forward toward the dash. He opened the hatch and pulled out the map. "I better make sure the house is empty." He opened it up and was probably searching through his coastline of numbers. With quick fingers, he shot off a text and not a minute later, his phone chimed.

"'K. The guy who owns the house said it's cool for us to use it tonight."

"Sweet." Saul lowered his visor against bright rays. "This Mowgli?"

"Yeah. Dude owes me a favor, too." Jake leaned forward to peer out the windshield. "Two miles to exit."

"Someone's antsy," Riley said dryly.

Saul let off the gas to merge with those getting off the highway. Out the western windows, the evening sun traced pink lines above the chalky sky. "Your old man doesn't sit still too well."

Jake told them to *watch it*, but there was a dash of humor to his voice. Riley adjusted his legs, unable to sit a minute longer himself. As the VW hit the exit and slowed, Riley looked over to a nearby stretch of beach parking. A barefoot guy sat on the bumper of an old Toyota truck playing a ukulele. Beside that, a bunch of kids piled sandy boogie boards into a minivan.

A few minutes later Saul and his dad were arguing about the exact location of the beach pad, and his dad proved to be correct when Riley spotted the "square white house" they'd all been looking for. Saul pulled up to the back of it and no one wasted a second climbing out of the van. Riley stood and arched his back to get some feeling into his legs. Jake went off to round up the hide-a-key. With a bear growl, Saul did a weird stretch-thing that scared a couple of seagulls away. Riley smiled and closed his door.

Not really sure what to do, he followed Saul around to the front of the house, and instantly his shoes sank into the sand. Saul kicked off his flip flops and trudged on. Riley pulled off his Converse and stuffed his socks inside before stashing them by the back stairs of the house. He followed Saul the short walk toward the water, savoring the cool sand on his feet and the crisp, salty breeze that hit his face.

Riley took a deep breath, letting it revive him.

A few body surfers and swimmers bobbed in the impact zone, and beyond that a handful of sailboats dotted the horizon like beads on a necklace. The sun hung low in the sky, making the water glitter and gray. He wished Becca were here to see it.

Key in hand, Jake joined them, and with Saul took a few minutes pointing to the water, analyzing the surf, cracking jokes. Finally, they started back the way they'd come. Riley followed his dad up the back steps to the lavish house. Two stories and a pristine white, the house looked more like modern art than anything else. Riley carried his shoes past the low glass wall that divided the lower deck from the beach and set them beneath a tiled dining table where a white canvas umbrella fluttered just above.

After unlocking the sliding glass door, Jake pushed it open. Inside, the air conditioning ran full blast, and the chilly air prickled Riley's skin. His dad shut down the AC, opened a couple of windows, then tossed the house key on the black granite countertop. With stainless steel appliances and leather furniture, Riley couldn't even begin to imagine the price tag on this place. Sure beat the motel he'd had in mind.

Saul declared himself on a mission to round up dinner.

"Hey and pick any of the rooms you want upstairs," Jake chimed in.

Wanting a shower, Riley lugged his things up the stark, white stairs and poked his head into a couple of rooms, finally picking a small one on the south corner with a view of the ocean. Better yet—the pier about a mile down the beach. He dropped his duffle and backpack, tugged out his shower stuff, and went in search of a bathroom.

Twenty minutes later, showered and shaved, he felt like a million bucks. Pushing his damp hair off to the side, he started down the stairs. His dad's cardboard box sat on the coffee table, and Saul stood at the door paying a delivery kid a handful of bills in exchange for some paper sacks. Based on the amazing smell—Chinese food. Riley pulled a stool up to the kitchen's bar and waited while Saul divvied up chow mein, egg rolls, and all kinds of other dishes Riley didn't recognize. In true Saul style, though, they looked amazing.

Just in case shellfish was in the mix, Riley stuck to teriyaki chicken and rice as he filled a plate.

Saul struggled to secure the lid on one of the Styrofoam containers. "See what we got to drink around here, will ya?" He tipped his head toward the fridge.

Riley opened the massive refrigerator and spied a couple of six packs of soda. He named the flavors.

"I'll have a cola." Saul took the red can and popped the top. "Grab a root beer for your dad."

Riley grabbed two and carried them to the bar. Starving, he speared a piece of meat, but Saul motioned toward the sliding glass doors.

"I think your old man just lit a fire."

They carried their plates to the back deck where just beyond, a fire crackled down on the beach. Jake was crouched in front of the pit, slowly feeding it small pieces of wood. He didn't come out of his quiet trance until Saul handed him a plate and fork.

"Thanks, man." He tipped his chin toward the sea. "*Ka makani 'olu 'olu.*"

Riley gave him one of the cold cans, then sat a few feet away. "What does that mean?" He hadn't heard Hawaiian spoken in a long time.

"It's your dad's way of saying 'a perfect wind,'" Saul answered.

Jake glanced over at Riley, dark eyes laced with regret. Maybe because it was a language Riley knew as a kid—but couldn't remember. Pulling his own gaze away, Riley pushed rice around with his fork. The sand was a strange kind of comfortable, and after sitting in a car all day, was pretty much the only spot he wanted to be right now. They ate without talking. After a while, the quiet mood energized when the two surfers got into a debate about something that happened in the '80s.

Having no idea what they were talking about, Riley collected the dishes and carried the stack into the house where he washed and dried everything. He really didn't want to sit around so he grabbed a beanie and slid it on as he headed back to the beach to stretch his legs. He tossed a wave to the guys and started toward the pier.

He slipped his hands in his pockets. The salty breeze rustled his black t-shirt. Little shells and pebbles lay scattered all around. He walked, and in the failing light, watched the sand for something he could bring Becca. A wet sand dollar poked up and Riley eased it loose. Broken. With a pitch of his arm, he flung it back to sea and walked on.

A few discoveries later, he found one that was perfectly round. The grainy, flat disc had a print in the center that almost looked like a flower. Riley turned it, and fearing it would break in his pocket, held it as he strolled down the shoreline. He didn't get far. The sun wouldn't be holding back the night much longer, and with the pier still far in the distance, Riley slowed to a stop and simply stared at the waves.

Water crashed and foamed. Retreated. Swelled. How many times had he listened to the sea while living in Orange County? The sound anything but calming. Anything but comforting. Now it was different.

At another sound rising...that of an acoustic

guitar…he looked farther down the beach. Riley walked on and cast a few glances toward a small group gathered around a bonfire. Some were singing. He eyed the cajón the drummer beat on, then realized that he recognized the song. It was one they'd just started learning at church.

Let go my soul and trust in Him…

The waves and wind still know His name.

The breeze pulled at Riley's hair, bringing with it those words and a sense that it was going to be okay. Right now he wasn't sure what *it* was, but it would probably look a heck of a lot like his dad climbing in that van and driving away. The day would come. And soon. Riley shifted his feet in the sand. Telling himself otherwise would do no good.

Expecting anything more from his dad would do no good.

Letting go… of what was and what wasn't and even what could be…

He had to. Riley listened to the campers as their song rose in the light of the setting sun. Everything else would be taken care of. His dad was a grown man. And based on his birth certificate, Riley was too. Come what may—Jake Kane would make a choice and he would have to do the same. What should have been scary, surprisingly wasn't.

Because not too long ago he'd sat in his living room thinking of all the things he'd done and regretted...

And asked God to come to his rescue.

Making him the son of a father who would never leave him.

Riley didn't really feel worthy—then or now—but maybe that was the whole point. He watched a few moments more, glancing from the guitar player, to the drummer, the singers, and finally back to the sea.

His phone beeped. He almost ignored the text, but maybe it was Becca. He checked and smiled.

My dad woke up! He's still in a lot of pain, though. :(With his leg broken the way it is, it will be a while until he can walk or drive. I think he might lose his job. It's okay...but he seems really down. He's worried about us, I think. We're going to be with him for a few hours, then head back to the campground. Did I tell you we got a spot? It has hookups and everything. Kind of far from the hospital, though. How are you doing? How is your time with your dad? Missing you like crazy.

Riley tapped Becca's name. It rang. *Answer, answer, answer...*

It went to her voicemail, which made sense if she was with her father. Pulling off his beanie, Riley spoke at the beep. "Hey, Becca. It's me." He turned some and plugged one ear against the offshore wind. "That's such good news about your dad!" Great. Now he was shouting. "I hope he can take it easy." Riley hadn't realized how windy it was until he'd started talking on the phone. "I miss you and I'll talk to you later." Maybe too loud. "Call me whenever you want. 'K. I love you. Bye." He hung up, then ninety watts of realization jolted his heart.

Oh, gosh.

He'd just told her he loved her. Actually he'd shouted it.

THIRTEEN

Shoot!

Riley stared at his phone.

She was going to think he was insane. Or worse, a creeper. "Just play it cool, man." That's all he could do at this point.

He started back the way he'd come. Riley smeared his hand over his forehead. He couldn't believe that had slipped out. Well, he could believe it, but he'd only been seeing her for a couple of weeks and the whole "I love you" thing was supposed to be a little while off. He'd totally jumped the gun. She'd get that message and probably have no idea what to say to him.

It was a good thing that he was alone because his face was on fire.

The sky was ash-black now, and Riley pulled his beanie back on as he trudged toward the little smudge of light that had to be his dad's fire. He checked his phone a dozen times from point A to point B, then finally made himself power it down and cram it in his back pocket before he lost his mind. Becca was with her dad and his little love fest explanation could wait.

The guys were gone, so Riley stood watching the flames by himself. It felt good, the quiet. Something he never thought he could like. There was a peace to just wind and earth and fire. No wonder his dad had piled wood and struck a match.

When the coals burned down to nothing other than a faint glimmer, Riley stepped away. Pretty sure half an hour had passed, he powered his phone back up but saw nothing other than the time and date. No missed anything. He headed up the stairs, and part of him wondered if he shouldn't just leave Becca another message…some kind of backtracking. Some way to amend what he'd said. But he couldn't bring himself to do it because he'd already spoken the truth with *I love you*. He'd never told a girl he loved her before. Not once. Let alone one that he'd never held and never kissed. He saw Becca's face in his mind. That dimpled smile, those brown eyes.

Remembered the very first day he'd seen her. Not on the side of the road surrounded by snow and Christmas trees. But years before—across that little table in Sunday school. He remembered those same eyes and smile. The little girl who'd given him her Dixie cup of water when he'd spilled his own. The one that didn't giggle with the others when the teacher had to wipe his jeans and shirt with paper towels.

The girl who sang "This Little Light of Mine" like there was no one else in the room.

And he just told her he loved her. He hoped she'd know it was for *all of it*.

Casting one last look to the black screen, an ache twisted in his heart as he stepped inside.

A hockey game belted from the huge flat screen in the living room and his dad and Saul took up opposite ends of the couch. Riley walked over. The cardboard box sat open—stacks of glossy postcards everywhere. The same size, and all photos of his dad, they were in neat piles according to the different images. Maybe five or six kinds. There had to be hundreds of cards if not more. Permanent marker in hand, Jake had his head bowed and signed one. Then another. And another.

His dark hair flopped down over his forehead and his brow was creased so tight that Riley wondered how long he'd been at this. Riley rested a hip on the arm of the sofa and just watched.

Saul muted the TV when commercials came on. He

tipped his chin in Riley's direction, then glanced to his buddy. "You almost done over there yet?"

"Not even close." Jake signed another, then tapped the small stack against the coffee table. He slid them onto a larger pile. Sitting up straighter, he peeled off his hooded sweatshirt and tossed it on the couch behind him. "Any chance you want to forge my signature?"

"Heck naw, brah. I already did mine." Saul shoved his wild hair back.

His dad looked to him and Riley held up his palms.

"Man, I need to find some new friends."

"How many of those do you have to sign?" Riley asked.

His dad lifted up a slip of paper and eyed it. "Packing slip says six hundred, so I'm gonna go with that."

"Seriously?" Riley moved around the coffee table to sit in the recliner that angled toward the TV. "All those are from your sponsor?"

"From one of 'em." Without looking up, Jake pulled an untouched stack closer, then scribbled his sloppy signature on the top card.

"Penance." Saul turned a silver ring on his thick pinkie.

"And you had to sign some too?" Riley asked.

Saul nodded toward one of the finished stacks. Riley realized it was the Mexican's picture. A shot of him flying a short board off the lip of a wave. The light of a rising sun made him and his board a cool, black silhouette.

"I didn't have as many because they like your dad more." Saul winked.

Jake snorted. "Yeah, right. I don't think 'like' would be the term just now." He signed two more cards.

Riley took one of the thick, glossy prints off Saul's stack. "Can I have one of these?"

Scribble, stack. Scribble, stack. His dad looked up. "What am I? Chopped liver?"

Not exactly. But each time Riley got one of his dad's letters as a kid, he'd wish the guy would get eaten by a shark.

Riley just gave him a muted smile. Saul took the postcard, popped the top off a marker, and thought for a second. He sketched out a funky little arrow then added a few words beneath that. Riley took the card back and read what Saul wrote.

Not all who wander are lost.

Riley grinned and thanked him. Holding the corners gingerly, he studied the image more closely. With Saul's hair shorter, the photo had probably been taken a few years ago. Riley planned to hang onto this.

His dad spared him a glance, then went back to signing. "Did you hear from Becca today?"

Riley set the card beside him. "She texted me."

"How's her dad doing?" Saul asked with a wince.

Riley filled them in on what he knew of the accident. How Jay Fletcher had swerved on instinct, avoiding a head-on with that family. All those kids. Saul listened soberly, and while the man with the marker kept at his work, Riley could tell he was listening too.

When Riley finished, Saul just shook his head gravely. "That's just..." His voice trailed off.

"You know—they should make these for truck drivers with six kids." Jake shook one of his signed cards then set it aside.

Riley's forehead pinched as he watched his dad.

Something deep and dark had flooded the man's eyes. "And I don't mean for penance. But if I were a kid...that's the kind of hero I'd want up on my wall."

Saul slowly nodded an agreement.

That look still in his eyes, Jake signed another card. Capped his marker. Then peered into the box and pulled out a new bundle. "I almost forgot." With his bare foot, he nudged a paper shopping sack beside the couch. "That's for you. It was in the box…they knew you were going to be with me."

"What is it?" Riley asked.

"I didn't open it." But the look on his face said he had a hunch.

Riley hefted the sack onto the couch cushion and peered inside. A stack of t-shirts sat neatly folded on top of some other stuff. One… two… three… four shirts. Riley pulled them out and set the pile aside. Below that was a hat. No, two. All with the price tags still on. At the very bottom of the bag sat a pair of skateboard trucks and a pack of wheels. The nicest he'd ever seen. Way better than what he had on his board.

"*Huh*," he said dumbly.

When a few seconds rolled by, his dad chuckled. "You know, most guys would be stoked right now. Stores don't just give merch to anybody. Especially the best stuff."

"It's just because I'm your son." How had Saul worded it? Mini-Me.

"No. It's because you're *really* good."

Riley slowly shook his head. He didn't want this. Not the stuff. Not the life. The expectations. He just wanted to be normal and everyday. "I like working at the feed store."

Saul and his dad exchanged a smile that was anything but judgmental.

"I guess I should tell them thank you."

Jake dipped his head. "Sure thing. Let me know if you want help."

Overwhelmed—and kind of feeling bad about not being more useful—Riley said goodnight and headed upstairs. He changed into sweats and stuffed his clothes in his bag. If he was smarter, he would have done a load of laundry while here. He spent some time trying to make sense of his mess. He folded clean clothes on one side of the bed and piled dirty laundry on the floor. Riley packed his duffle back up the best he could, then decided it was time to stop stalling.

He'd heard Saul go to bed... and could still hear a rustling coming from downstairs. Which meant his dad was still up.

Not really wanting to put on a shirt, Riley just tied the string on his sweatpants and started back down the stairs. Jake was in the same spot on the couch. Stacks of unsigned postcards still covered the coffee table. The black marker squeaked across a photo, then several more.

Riley came around the couch and his dad glanced up.

Surprise quirked his brow. "Hey."

"Hey." Riley moved the packing slip and sat.

"I take it you're not here to forge."

"Actually, I'm kind of thinking about it…."

"But?"

Riley folded the packing slip. Unfolded it. "I dunno…some kid's gonna get one of those and believe it's the real deal. I could fake it…but I guess they deserve better than that, you know?" He picked up a postcard and held it gingerly in his fingertips. "I'd want better. The real deal." He looked over at his dad who gave a sad smile.

The picture in hand was one of his dad sitting on a beach at sunset. All alone, with a board behind him. It was a stunning sky and his dad looked totally cool, but Riley didn't like the aloneness of it. Another stack showed a picture of him grinning, flashing hang-loose fingers. It was almost the same smile from that old picture from Yosemite. But not as big.

Riley picked one of those up. "Can I have this?"

"You don't have to—"

"I want to."

His dad lifted a shoulder in a shrug, but his face looked anything but indifferent. "If you want."

Riley nodded slowly, staring back to the glossy print.

He traced his finger over the signature and thought of the cards his dad had sent him over the years. All the ones he'd trashed. Something inside him ached over that. Ached in a way that he couldn't even explain.

"Thanks."

Jake dipped his head. "I'll try and think of something cool to add like Saul."

Surprised, Riley nodded. "Okay. Thanks." Then he realized that he was doing nothing but holding up the operation. Pressing hands to knees, he rose. Riley held the postcard carefully. "I'll see you in the morning." He motioned with the card, then headed for the stairs.

"Say…"

He turned. "Yeah?"

"I was thinking about something." Jake ran his eyes against his shoulder and looked tired. "It's about Jay. Him and his family. I was thinking about all they're going through and wondering about helping them out maybe."

Riley nodded.

"I don't think they'd want a handout, and I don't blame them. But I thought maybe some kind of fundraiser. Like a surf camp for a week or something. Rent a couple spots at one of the campgrounds on the coast. And if you'd be up for it, maybe you could run some kind of skate clinic for kids." He shrugged. "I've been a part of them before, though I've never put one together. They seem to do pretty well."

Riley had no idea what to say.

"We could talk to Jay, see what he thought. Maybe Becca could help out. I dunno..." Jake smirked. "Her mom could do KP or something. Make snacks for all the kids signed up. That way the Fletchers could all be involved, and maybe raising money that way would feel more comfortable for them. What do you think?"

Riley pinched the card tighter in his hand. Stared at the man who just made him speechless.

"Did you catch all that or should I say it again?"

Riley smiled. "I think I caught it this time. And...that sounds great." He blinked quickly, trying not to show his shock. "I think Becca and her family will be thrilled."

His dad dipped his head, looking glad himself. "You can talk to them, then? And we'll set something up for this summer?"

"It's a deal." Riley patted a hand against the frame of the doorjamb. "Thanks, Dad. I really appreciate that."

"You got it."

FOURTEEN

Riley woke to the sound of voices. Chatter that wasn't all that…distant. With morning light flooding his room, he thought instantly of Becca and grabbed his phone. But still nothing.

Nothing?

Blowing out a breath, he sat up and untangled himself from the sheets. He walked over to the window to peer down. The sky was cloudy and so overcast that he half expected to see drops on the wooden deck below. A dozen yards beyond, in front of the beach house, were ten people—easy—even though a glance at the clock showed it wasn't even seven. The mixture of guys and girls were clad in jeans and sweaters. A few wore wetsuits. But what were they doing standing in front of the beach house, watching the ocean?

Riley lifted his gaze to see a surfer paddling for a growing swell on the water. He knew in an instant that it was his dad. Leaning on the windowsill, Riley watched as the man caught the wave. Knees bent, Jake carved down and ran his hand along the small barrel that glinted in the morning light.

It took Riley a minute to throw on jeans and a hoodie before starting downstairs. At the smell of coffee, he filled a cup, added enough creamer to give any decent barista a heart attack, then stepped out onto the deck. Mug in hand, Saul was leaning on the rail, watching the commotion. The cross in his ear caught the sunrise when he glanced Riley's way.

"Have they never seen someone surf before?" Riley asked, taking the same position.

Saul chuckled. "You don't make the cover of Sports Illustrated three times without this kind of thing happening." His mop-top flopped in the breeze as he sipped from his mug. "Comes with the territory, *mijo*." Saul slid a wink in Riley's direction. "We better hit the road, though." The hulky guy straightened and threw back the last of his coffee. "Grub's on the counter. I just hit the farmer's market so help yourself."

"Thanks."

Saul squeezed Riley's shoulder, then stepped into the house.

Wanting a better gauge on how long this was going

to last, Riley started down the stairs. To the north, thick clouds were rolling in, and while a chill hung in the air, the beach was still bright. As he passed along the crowd, he watched his dad paddle back out. A few other surfers bobbed beyond the impact zone, straddling boards. His dad joined them, and from their body language they all chatted easily. Riley tried to imagine being in their place. Wondered what it would be like to head out at dawn, thinking this would be a morning like any other, only to bump into one of the most famous surfers in the world.

"You with Jake Kane?" someone asked beside him.

Riley glanced over to see a middle-aged, petite woman. "You could say that."

Her blonde hair was pulled back in a ponytail and she looked just like his second-grade teacher. Except she angled to the ocean, lifted a camera with a huge lens, and snapped it three times. "You his son? You look just like him." She smiled in a friendly way.

Riley nodded a little. "I didn't think so many people would want to come out and watch him."

She looked amused by that. "Well, I was across the street having breakfast when someone came in saying he was here. A few of us walked over to check it out. The crowd grew from there."

Glancing around, Riley realized that the crowd had doubled now. People stood in groups. A few surfers who were soaked and carrying boards, likely heading back to their cars, had stopped to watch as well.

"I'm still kind of in shock." She snapped several more pictures. "I've been following your dad's career for years."

When a fresh set of waves rolled in, most of the surfers started paddling. After a few strokes, his dad slowed and sat back, letting one of the rookies take the wave. The kid bombed, which made everyone laugh, including the photographer lady.

"That one needs a bit of practice," Riley chuckled. "Maybe my dad will give him pointers."

"It'd be just like him to."

Folding his arms over his chest, Riley locked in on the kid who was trying to get back on his board. With determined strokes, he paddled back out. It took a couple of minutes for him to get free of the impact zone, and this time the lanky teen settled on his board away from the rest of the group. Riley's dad paddled over. He floated up beside the teen and sat up, adjusting his straddle on the surfboard. Jake talked easily with the kid for a minute, and was soon using hand motions to probably illustrate some technique. The kid nodded to everything he said.

Riley just watched.

"I'm still trying to figure out why he's not in Hawaii," the blonde woman blurted. "When someone said they spotted him here on dawn patrol, I had to see for myself."

"What do you mean?"

"Haven't you ever heard of the Wave of the Winter?"

"What's that?"

"Are you serious?" She snapped another picture, then looked over at Riley—her expression not unkind—only curious.

"Uh...yeah."

The woman reached back to adjust her ponytail. "Wow."

"I'm not really that into surfing," Riley said dryly.

"Okay." She gave him a friendly glance.

"So what is this Wave of the...?"

"Winter. It's a competition that started up a couple years ago. All the greatest surfers who can afford to hit the North Shore to battle for the sickest wave of the winter." The lady popped the lens off her camera and tucked the attachment into the black case draping her shoulder. "Whoever gets it, wins twenty-five grand."

Riley tipped his chin.

"Not that a guy like your dad needs the money or anything. But the title's impressive—some serious bragging rights. He's won it once already." She put on a different lens and fast-clicked the shutter. The light dimmed as the clouds moved closer. "I can't believe he's not there right now. This is the sweet spot of the season on Oahu. He's insane to be surfing five-foot waves in Santa Barbara when everyone else is hitting twenty-foot barrels on the Island." Her tanned brow furrowed. "All the magazines made it sound like he was gonna be there."

Riley peeled his gaze away from the photographer. His dad was just catching a wave, lifting onto his feet…to a stand. He whipped his board back, curled it around, then whipped it again. All with expert ease and precision. Riley had to admit—the guy had some serious style.

The lady beside him snapped a few quick pictures before saying something about a bit of gold for the local paper. "But there's gonna be some bummed-out fans on Oahu this month."

"Maybe he didn't want to go this year." Riley told the lady about the competition his dad and Saul had coming up in Texas.

"Texas? Wave snobs like your dad *don't* do

tournaments down there." She let out a giggle that didn't match her know-it-all facts. "He surfs Australia and the North Shore Pipeline. If he was heading to Texas, it wouldn't be for much other than crawfishing."

What? Riley looked back at Jake who jumped off his board, vanishing feet first into the froth.

Realizations slapping heat to his skin, Riley reached back and tugged his sweater up his back, pulling it over his head and off. His shirt accidentally rode up with it. The woman watched him curiously as he tugged it back into place.

"*What's your name?*"

He hesitated. "Riley."

She mouthed the words, Riley Kane. "That's right. I've heard of you. I mean, everyone knows he has a son, but you keep a pretty low profile." Her brow pinched and her gaze roved as if she was trying to read something written on him. "How long are you gonna be in town for? Any chance I could get a couple shots for one of the teen magazines. The girls would be all over—"

"Maybe another time." Overwhelmed, he stepped away, and while his dad got swarmed by onlookers, Riley tried to get a handle on the misfiring in his brain.

One guy held out a board to be autographed. A girl

asked the still-dripping pro to sign the sleeve of her pink wetsuit. A dozen more signatures and a couple of obligatory photos later, Jake started at a little jog for the beach house. Riley stepped back to let him pass, then trailed him up the steps.

Inside, his dad closed the slider, turned the lock, and lowered the blinds. "What do you say we all get out of here?" he asked with an animated bob to his eyebrows.

Saul gave him a curious look that said a million things Riley couldn't begin to decipher.

Riley tried to say something, but nothing came. He didn't even know where to begin. What was this business with the North Shore? His dad was supposed to be there right now—he suddenly knew it for a fact. Rushing his mind was the memory of canceled plane tickets and the man leaning over a map of Hawaii. The Weather Channel, phone calls with sponsors...signing postcards as penance.

Riley swallowed hard, having no idea what was going on or why his dad was here with him when he should be somewhere else.

"Hey." With a good-natured shuck to Riley's chin, Jake got his attention. "You want to stand there like a fish with your mouth open or hit the road?"

Dipping his head, Riley started for the stairs. "I'll

just get my stuff." In his room, he sat on the bed and used his phone to pull up the news feed. Riley hashtagged #waveofthewinter, scrolling through the posts for some clue as to what was going on. When his screen exploded with pictures of insane waves and predictions on who would win the twenty-five grand, he searched for his dad's name instead. #jakekane.

And there it was.

Everyone in the surfing world. Wondering where on earth he was.

FIFTEEN

Riley's ten-minute crash course about the competition taught him a few critical facts. For one, the contest only ran from November to February, which meant it ended in just a couple of weeks. Two, the challenge was cutthroat. Taking place over one of the fiercest reefs on the shoreline, only the best of the best went out there and lived to tell the tale. Whoever was crowned victor earned the title through a heck of a lot of work among the most prestigious waves in the world. And third, that lady had been wrong.

It was pretty much the only competition his dad had never won.

"Gonna listen to your book on tape?"

Having spent the last twenty minutes staring out his window at the rain, Riley glanced over at his dad in the driver's seat. "Naw. I guess I'll wait for Saul to wake up so he doesn't miss anything." Riley had been working at the bent nails but was nowhere near to solving the puzzle so he tossed them down on his backpack.

The side of his dad's mouth slid up. "You two are a hoot with that children's book."

"I suppose it's a good story." Riley peered through the windshield where the wipers worked overtime. "Saul's really into it. I think he teared up yesterday when the boy walked down off his mountain looking for another human to talk to."

Finally heading east, the van spritzed down the wet freeway, the ocean at their backs, New Mexico a couple of days ahead.

Elbow propped up on the door, Jake ran a hand over his mouth. "Saul's a good guy."

Slowly, Riley nodded. "How long have you two been friends?"

Jake stared out the rain-splattered windshield. "A *long* time." His expression went nostalgic. "I met him in Queensland, Australia. We were just two seventeen-year-old rookies who had no idea what we were doing. For both of us, it was our first year on the junior pro circuit. I'd never been anywhere but the Islands, and Saul, he was just a poor kid from Baja, California. We were in the same heat and nearly killed one another. I cut him off at least twice and dropped in on his best wave, winning first place by a couple of points.

"I thought when we got back to the beach he was gonna punch my face in, but he just walked over while I was packing up and asked if I wanted to grab something to eat. He's been my best buddy ever since."

Riley smiled.

"Guy's one of the finest people I've ever met. He's the best surfer I know, too."

"But you're better ranked than him?"

"Yeah...well. Ranking's not everything. I just happened to have some good waves at good times. When it comes to the everyday...to life..." He glanced at the rearview mirror that showed Saul asleep in the middle seat. "That man out-surfs me ten to one."

Riley turned to see Saul with a wadded up Mexican blanket under his head for a pillow. Dude was out.

"To Saul, surfing is so complex." Jake adjusted the heater, turning up the knob. Warm air blasted from the vents. "To that man, it's about being out there in the waves. It's about the sunrise. The water. To Saul, surfing's not a competition...it's a celebration."

Riley shifted his vent, then studied his dad's expression.

"It's something I'm finally beginning to catch on to.

I wish I would have done it a lot sooner."

Riley pulled off his baseball cap, scratched his head, and adjusted the hat back over his hair. "Would you give up your titles to go back?" He shaped the bill of his cap, realizing there was so much in that question. The question he'd wanted to ask his dad every day of his life for as long as he could remember.

The man looked at him. Pierced him straight through with a steely gaze…then nodded as he looked back to the road. "I would."

Swallowing hard, Riley fiddled with a tear in the knee of his jeans. He cleared his throat, having no idea what to say to that or how to say it. Finally, with a weak voice, he said, "You should call Mom sometime."

"I call your mom all the time."

Riley peered over at his dad.

"She has selective answering skills. Has for years." He let off the clutch and downshifted when the rain picked up speed. "She's smart like that," he said softly.

Hitching one of his shoes over the other, Riley nudged his knees against the passenger door. He leaned his head against the cool glass of the window. Arms folded over his chest, he settled in, thinking that if he could get lost in the scenery whizzing by, he wouldn't have to continue down this road of trying to make sense of any of this. His mom. His dad.

Why he was starting to give a rat about the guy beside him.

Everything.

"So what about you? What have you been up to the last couple of years?"

Riley blinked a few times at his dad's sudden curiosity.

"What do you do? Where do you work? Tell me about your friends. And your girl."

Riley shifted to sit up more. "That's a lot in one question."

"We've got some time on our hands." He flashed that smile again.

Pulling his cap off, Riley shaped the bill more, folding it in his hands as he thought. "Let's see...the girl, as you know, is Becca, and I've been seeing her for a little while."

"The homeschooled girl."

"Yeah."

"She nice?"

"She's really nice."

"And I know you've gotta have about fifty pictures

of her, so let's see."

Riley scrolled through his camera roll and tried not to notice that there were no missed calls or texts from her. He found a picture of him and Becca sitting on the edge of her porch, Christmas lights and snow behind them. Bundled in coats and beanies, they'd sat there talking for hours on New Year's Eve. At midnight, instead of trying to get a kiss, he'd pulled out his phone and snapped the shot. Becca was beaming and he looked just as happy.

His dad glanced at it a couple times. "She's cute. Looks really sweet."

Riley studied her face, missing her so much it hurt.

"You met her working, you said?"

"Yeah. I work at a small feed store. Harmony Farms. It's up in the mountains near Idyllwild. Mom and I lived there for a couple of years when I was little."

His dad's expression went bittersweet. "I remember that."

"I worked there as a volunteer for a few winters when I was sixteen and seventeen, selling Christmas trees during school break. Some kind of work release community service thing I had to do '*to learn responsibility,* '" he added with air quotes. "It was kind of a drive, but I'd always liked it there and moved back after graduation. The man who owns the store, Mr. Lawrence, gave me a full-time job and helped me find a cheap place to live. It's a cramped little cabin, but it works." Riley shrugged. "As for friends, I've got a few good ones these days. But when I was younger...I didn't exactly have a Saul."

Jake gave him a bittersweet smile.

"I had a bunch of buddies in Orange County, but I wasn't very good at picking winners, if you know what I mean." Riley looked over at his dad. "Just got in a lot of trouble that I ended up having to pay for." Starting over hadn't been easy, but he was trying to do it carefully.

Jake tapped his thumb on the steering wheel a couple of times. "About that trouble you got into. Mind if I ask how that all happened?"

"Uh..." Riley looked up as they drove under an overpass with a huge green sign declaring that they were still on the I-40. "I got caught ripping off a convenience store. It wasn't the first time I'd done it. I was fifteen, so they went easy on me, I guess, by not sending me to juvie. Mom and I had to pay some fines and I had to do a whole bunch of community service. There was also some other stuff in my file, so I ended up having to take classes. Anger Management 101." Riley made a face. "That's what I called it." He fiddled with the hole in his jeans again.

"Why did you do it?" his dad asked.

"I dunno." When his dad waited, Riley tried to elaborate. "Stealing's kind of a natural high. It's sorta thrilling. Like you're on top of the world."

"For stealing Twinkies?"

Riley chuckled. "Well, when you put it that way." He laughed again. "And I never stole any Twinkies." Just stuff he could use himself or sell. Sobering a little, he shrugged one shoulder. "Mr. Lawrence...him and his wife were so nice to me. I mean, what if some punk walked into their little store and ripped them off? I'd want to clobber him." He shrugged again, the simple motion feeling too small. "It made me realize that I had let myself become someone that I didn't even like."

His dad nodded slowly, a shadow across his brow.

"Mom put up with a lot because of me. I don't know if things are going perfect, but the last couple of years, we've been on the up and up and she's been awesome the whole time."

"I'm glad to hear it." His dad flashed him a muted smile that looked weighed down by regrets of his own. "That hard work you've been doing...it shows. I hope you know that."

"Thanks." Riley glanced out to the ugly, tan wall that edged this stretch of highway. Tired of graffiti and cracks in the concrete, he dug his iPod and headphones from his bag and turned on some music. He closed his eyes, thinking to steal a couple of z's before he'd need to drive again. Saul would wake up soon and was going to be useless until he had coffee, so it would likely be Riley's turn next. He was three songs into his chillstep mix when his cell buzzed in his pocket.

Riley checked the screen. It was Becca. A gloriously long text about how she and her mom had been so busy with her dad waking up, that they had forgotten their chargers in his hospital room. The batteries had fizzled out before they realized, but they now had them back. She finished by thanking him for his message. Followed by tons of hearts. Riley grinned and read the message two more times.

I have something to tell you, she added.

His mouth tipped up and he started to ask what it was when a text flashed through.

Aloha wau ia 'oe.

Riley grinned again. *What does that mean?*

You don't speak Hawaiian?

No. My mom wouldn't let me.

His phone vibrated again when she sent a text back. *Oh my gosh, I feel horrible.*

Don't feel bad! Stand by. For a second Riley thought about asking his dad, but typed in *I'm gonna Google it.* He pulled up the internet and pasted in the phrase. Searching proved slow with the lack of Wi-Fi and the heavy rain. The search icon kept turning and turning, and not wanting to keep Becca waiting, Riley cleared his throat.

"Say, what does aloha-waaaauuu-ia-oooo mean?"

His dad chuckled. "*Aloha wau ia 'oe*?"

"Yeah, that's it."

"It means 'I love you.'"

Riley sat up so fast he nearly smacked his head. "Holy bajeebers."

The van swerved, but his dad righted the wheel. "What's the matter?"

"Nothing." Riley chuckled. "Hold on."

His thumbs hovered over the keypad as he tried to think of how to respond. It needed to be something really good. Or poignant. But all he could think of was thank you. After a deep breath, he typed that in. He sent it off, then added, *you're a brave soul.* His heart beat away the seconds—certain there was no way she could have meant that—until she responded.

YOU are a brave soul. And I mean it.

Why did she believe in him so much? His chest constricting, Riley cleared his throat. People didn't love him. Not unless they had to or were obligated to. Even that was optional. Throat tight, he read her messages again, smiling like an idiot to himself.

"That your girl?" his dad asked.

Nodding, Riley lifted his head and peered out the windshield where a bit of sun was beginning to poke through the clouds.

With a grin, his dad reached over and nudged Riley's shoulder with a fist. "You got stars in your eyes, son."

SIXTEEN

The kid spoke—well, the narrator.

And the story had become so engaging that as Riley glanced at the van's speaker, he could practically see this boy standing in the woods, meeting the strange man who had wandered past his treehouse in the wilderness. Pretty sure he was a bandit on the run from the police, the kid nicknamed him *Bando.*

That was kind of funny.

The boy said that he didn't know anything about the stranger and that the stranger didn't know anything about him but that he could stay there if he wanted to.

A kind of hospitality that had Riley blinking—wondering if he would do the same.

The boy went on to offer the man supper. The food that he'd caught or collected with his own two hands. All that he'd toiled to save and gather over his lonely summer months.

Riley leaned back against the driver's seat. Saul

turned up the volume on the after-market CD player.

The boy offered the bandit his choice of venison or rabbit.

Bando…sounding surprised by such generosity… asked for venison.

Suddenly, Jake lunged from the center seat and hit pause. "Wait, what is venison and who is this other guy again?"

"The boy found him in the woods, remember?" Saul said from the copilot's seat. "Thinks he's running away from the cops. And venison is deer meat. You need to get out more."

Riley adjusted the rearview mirror and glimpsed his dad.

"Besides, I thought you didn't care," Saul added.

Doing a bad job of looking like he didn't, Jake leaned back again. Saul told him to put his seatbelt on.

Riley tapped play and the narrator's voice filled the interior again. The boy explained how the stranger watched as he lit a fire with flint and steel. The kid got the fire blazing, and the stranger was enamored with what he'd just done. Before much could be said, the falcon flew down from her perch, making the outlaw jump.

The boy introduced his feathered friend, Frightful.

Riley's dad reached forward and hit pause again. "Who names a falcon Frightful? And isn't the dad going to show up any second?"

"*Pshht*." Saul reached back and socked him in the leg. "You're ruining the story for others in the car, *vato*."

A wadded up piece of paper pelted Saul in the head.

"Am I the only one who hasn't read this?" Riley asked, glancing in the mirror again.

"Don't worry." His dad pulled sunglasses from the neck of his shirt and slipped them on. "I seriously can't remember anything."

"Then hold still and keep quiet and you won't have so many questions," Saul said.

"And put your seatbelt on." Riley tapped play.

His dad buckled up as the narrator started again.

Out the window, shrubby trees lined the side of the road. Fields of dry grasses, and beyond that, grayish hills and mountains. They didn't pause the CD again until an hour down the road when Saul muted everything to remind Riley to just stay on the 40 through Flagstaff. Which would have been no problem if traffic wasn't packed. Whether a fender bender or just the city itself, something had clogged the roadway and the speedometer wouldn't hit twenty miles per hour.

Nearly to a stop, Riley glanced over his shoulder to see his dad twisting the bent nails. The guy kept looking from cars to road signs and all around. Antsy. Riley thought of the boards strapped to the top of the van and how for one of the few times in his dad's life, he was landlocked.

And then some. Riley thought of the Wave of the Winter that his dad was missing. Probably best to ask about it when he had him alone. Riley would bring it up tonight.

Jake rested an arm on the back of his seat. "Let's just stick with this until dark. Get as far as possible. Then we can snag a hotel. Cool with you, guys?"

Riley and Saul chimed in that it was fine with them.

Needing a change of pace, Riley turned on the radio and scrolled back and forth until he found a classic rock station. Saul tapped his flip flop against the floorboard and Riley drummed a thumb between *ten and two* on the steering wheel. Up ahead the traffic was clearing. Maybe they were all antsy, because five minutes later, between him on the steering wheel and Saul pounding the passenger side door, they pretty much had the drums to Tom Petty's "American Girl" worked out. More than a little into it, Riley glanced over to see a car full of teen girls giggling at them. One even blew a kiss.

He stopped his stupid banging and tried to play it cool by flashing a peace sign with the back of his hand. The commotion in the girl car animated. Embarrassed for all eternity, he let off the gas so they flew past.

His dad laughed a laugh Riley hadn't heard since he was a kid. Saul nudged his shoulder, said some quip in Spanish, and despite it all—or maybe *because* of it all— Riley felt a strange kind of happy. The border sign for New Mexico zipped by. With dusk settling, a glance at the GPS showed that they had only five hours until Taos. Which meant they'd arrive tomorrow. He was almost to her.

His dad, who had been watching signs like a hawk, pointed out a family-style hotel. Once they hit the off ramp, Riley slid his window farther open. Early evening air poured in—a sweet mixture of fading desert warmth and distant rain.

"I need to mail these postcards," Jake said, pointing to a strip mall as they passed it. "You guys park, then I'll come back to that shipping joint."

Riley turned the van into the hotel roundabout. He and Saul climbed out and grabbed their bags while his dad slid into the driver's seat. Hitching the strap of his duffle over his shoulder, Riley trailed Saul into the hacienda-style lobby. They booked a room, then hauled their stuff up to the third floor. When Jake joined them, they all stood staring at the two queen beds.

"I'm so not about to cuddle with either one of you." Jake sat and plucked up the hotel phone.

Five minutes later, a cot was brought up for the guy who could probably have just booked the whole hotel. While his dad got domestic with sheets and pillows, Riley headed out to try and burn off energy. Otherwise he wouldn't be sleeping that night, comfy bed or not. He headed down the final flight of stairs and snagged the skateboard off the roof rack of the van. As he rode in the back parking lot, clouds dragged across the purple sky. He ollied over a broken parking block, getting higher and higher each time, until the manager came out a side door and told him to knock it off.

Used to the drill, Riley apologized, clutched up the board, and climbed the stairs, looking for door 312. He let himself in and pocketed the key.

"So here's the plan." Saul sat on the bed in a hooded sweater and jeans where he flipped through a travel brochure. "A few blocks down is a drive-in movie theatre. Show already started, but they've got a bunch of street vendors for some event they've got going on. By the list, it's guaranteed to be some seriously good eats. I follow one of these joints on Instagram and have been dying to try their tacos. We could drive, but if you're all up for being cold, I say we walk."

"I'm in." Riley dug through his duffle for a sweatshirt.

He bumped Becca's sand dollar which was wrapped in a t-shirt. He carefully set the bundle back on top of his stuff where it wouldn't get crushed. Stealing a squeeze of his dad's mousse, Riley stood in front of the bathroom mirror and made his hair do something nice, taking too long, he realized, when Saul whistled a catcall as the guys headed out.

Riley followed them down to the street just as the first stars glinted overhead. Stoplights flashed red, green, and yellow, and a flock of birds moved slowly on the horizon. At the crosswalk, Saul popped a piece of gum from a plastic pack. He'd gotten it at the last gas station, but Riley hadn't been paying attention. Now he glimpsed the label and realized it was the kind to help quit smoking.

Saul rubbed at his head as if it hurt. Riley remembered that ache.

"If you can do it, kid..." Saul elbowed him.

Riley tapped a fist against Saul's tight shoulder. "You got this."

Walking the few blocks to the drive-in felt like heaven. Even before they passed under the archway advertising *The Princess Bride* tonight, the sights and sounds of a ton of people in cars and trucks drew them closer. Not to mention the smell of fried food. Was that…funnel cake? Riley ran a hand down his stomach. Couples wove hand-in-hand between vehicles, while families were snuggled into the beds of pickup trucks with blankets and popcorn. The Cliffs of Insanity flashed on the giant screen as the actors started up the thick rope.

The line for Saul's dream tacos was insane, so Saul offered to stand in it. Riley and his dad handed over tens along with their orders and the big guy sent them off with a thumbs-up.

Riley walked with his dad toward the back of the sitting area where picnic tables were already half filled with diners. Jake chose a grassy spot beside a tree where he could lean and nudge his baseball cap farther back. A strategic kind of discreet that Riley knew he lived with every day. Riley straddled the bench on the opposite side. They watched the movie in silence for a while, and by the time the sword fight was in full swing, Saul carried over cardboard boxes of food.

He handed each of them a root beer, then stretched out on the grass in front of the tree. Saul watched the screen through that scene and into the next. He sipped from his soda and kept mouthing the lines to the movie. Even the girl parts.

Riley smirked in his dad's direction.

Jake chuckled. "Wasn't this Isabel's favorite?" he asked Saul.

Saul smiled in a way Riley had never seen before.

"Who's Isabel?" Riley asked.

He must have said it too softly, because Saul was still in movie mode.

His dad answered in a low voice. "Saul's wife."

"He's married?"

One side of his dad's face scrunched, and Riley had to strain to hear his words. "She passed away a couple years ago."

Lounging on his side, Saul watched the film with rapt attention. Riley glanced back to his dad who wore an expression so pained, it declared just how much the woman—Isabel—meant to them.

"I didn't realize…"

"I just didn't mention it, I guess." Jake popped the

metal top off his soda bottle. "They'd dated since they were kids practically. Got married at nineteen. I was the best man in their wedding."

Saul tipped his head back and spoke. "*Best* best man a guy could have."

Riley felt a sad smile surface then looked to his dad. "And he was in yours, wasn't he?"

A nod. "Couple of years later."

"It was on the beach."

He nodded again…the look in his eyes a few notches heavier than bittersweet.

"I saw a picture once." Found in a shoebox under his mom's dresser, the faded image was the only one Riley had ever seen of that day. Though he had never put two and two together before, he realized that Saul was in the photo.

"You wore that cute little suit." Saul made the motion of a bowtie and grinned back at Riley.

"I was *there*?"

His dad nodded like it was the last thing in the world he wanted to do.

"I thought you got married before I was born."

He shook his head. "Not until you were two." Soda bottle in hand, he spoke to it instead of Riley. "That's when I settled down and we all moved to O.C."

Settled down? He didn't even want to think about what that meant. Riley pushed away his box of food. He wiped his fingers on a napkin for the sole purpose of pulling his gaze away. "Are there any other little Kanes out there that I should know about?"

"No. Just you."

Appetite gone, he wanted to pitch his dinner, but with the taco already dripping in his hand, Riley made himself take another bite. He chewed, swallowed, and felt sick. "Why did you even bother staying? Why marry her if you didn't mean it?"

A muscle in his dad's jaw twitched. He swigged from his drink and the look was gone. "I'd made it clear I wasn't ready to get married so she stayed in Cali because she was still at the university and needed her mother's help with you."

Riley stared at the space between them.

"Your mom was doing a million things on her own, but I just couldn't pull myself away from surfing—the rankings—and trying to stay on top." Jake rubbed a hand over his forehead. "I used to visit the two of you whenever I could get to the area, and by the time she had graduated, I'd burned through her trust. I was losing the both of you." He moved his box of food in front of him but didn't seem all that interested in eating either. He glanced over, brow pressed down. "On one of those visits, you were just this little runt that followed me everywhere. You were toddling around and asking a billion questions that I couldn't understand. You were all lispy and drooly, and you took hold of my thumb in your little hand the moment I got there and you wouldn't let it go." Head back, the lights from the movie reflected in his dark brown eyes. "And I...I just couldn't get on that plane again."

At least not that time.

Maybe he was thinking the same thing.

Knowing he needed to chill out, Riley absently took a bite, not tasting a thing. Getting mad at his dad right now wasn't going to fix anything. He made himself speak calmly—willing that calm to settle inside him. "How old were you when you married Mom?"

"I think I was twenty-four."

Twenty-two when he was born then. "And you just married her because you had to." Probably not the nicest question to ask. But he *did* say it calmly at least.

The wince that followed looked like it wasn't for Jake's sake. "I didn't have to do anything. I actually adored her."

Riley swallowed hard. For so many reasons. "So you just left because of me." He wondered how long it took for that hand-over-thumb magic to wear off.

His dad shook his head so deliberately that Riley couldn't look away. "I left because of me."

With a knowing glance, Saul rose, trash in hand.

"I wanted to try and be a real dad. And I did it for a couple years. But...there was a huge part of me that was insanely selfish." He rubbed the sole of his shoe against the grass underfoot, gaze following. A lock of black hair fell across his forehead. "For years, I kept trying to be the dad I was supposed to be...and you and your mom...the two of you had me wanting to try—"

Which was the biggest bunch of baloney Riley had ever heard.

Stay calm.

Saul came back. Suddenly remembering the saucy taco dripping in his hand, Riley crammed more into his mouth just to try and be rid of it. He hadn't really noticed the flavor of the meat yet and got an odd taste. "So why did she tell me to call you?" he mumbled.

"She and I had been talking off and on and she knew I wanted to try and be—"

"Saul?" Riley swallowed. His stomach suddenly turning inside out, he looked at the tiny portion of taco still in his fingers. He opened up the tortilla and nudged aside the cilantro and salsa to check the meat. "What kind of tacos are these?"

"I got you chicken."

"Are you sure?"

"Positive. I made sure and asked for *only chicken*."

Riley blew out a slow breath as his dad took the wrapper and studied the contents.

"That's not chicken." Jake pushed the toppings aside. "It's shrimp."

Riley's heart ratcheted.

"Why did you eat the whole thing?" His dad rose and came around to Riley's side of the table.

"I wasn't paying attention!"

"It's just the one, right? You'll be okay?"

Riley swallowed hard, trying to think of where his EpiPen was. "I'm going to need my shot." His voice felt numb. Distant.

Because he knew what was about to happen.

Saul rose. "Where is it?"

"In my bag." Riley cleared his throat but it was already starting to itch. And he needed to find a bathroom.

Now. He coughed into his hand. "There's a big, clear Ziploc. It's in there in the bottom somewhere. The shot is long with a yellow label and…" he coughed again, "an orange cap."

Saul took off and Jake called for him to hurry. Riley said he was going to hurl and his dad led him over to the nearby concrete building where they barged into the men's room. Riley barely got to a stall before he lost his cookies. The sound of running water, then wet paper towels were passed his way. Riley spent the next five minutes on his knees—vowing to never eat again—grateful the bathroom was empty.

By the time he finally made it back outside, a few wide-eyed onlookers had to part for them. His dad led him back to their spot under the tree. Reaching it, Riley sank down in the grass and tried to catch his breath.

His dad knelt in front of him. "What about some water? What should I do?" An edge sharpened his voice. "Should I take you to the doctor or something?"

If his mom were here, she'd have already called an ambulance."Um…" Riley's heart hammered in his chest. He drew in another inhale and already it was difficult. "You should probably call 911."

His dad punched numbers into his phone.

Riley heard him talking as one minute dragged from five to eternity. Riley blinked over and over. His eyelids stung and tingled which meant they were swelling. Not good. That's when Riley remembered that the hotel key was still in his pocket. "For crying out loud." He growled at his own stupidity.

Riley struggled to pull the plastic card out and someone ran off with it in the direction Saul had gone. Riley prayed that Saul had found a way in already.

"I need the shot right now," Riley said. He should have carried the injector on him always like the doctor told him to. His throat closed tighter. Another dose of panic spit fire into his veins. "*Right* now." Out of desperation, his hand moved to his stomach where the vial used to live strapped there as a kid. Nothing.

Because now he just took to having it *around*.

And now it was expired.

His dad knelt beside him. He looked back the way Saul had vanished across the street. "Saul will be back in just a sec." His voice seemed far away.

Hands starting to shake, Riley gripped his dad's forearm. He squeezed his burning eyes closed. His tongue didn't want to move. "Did you call 911?" he whispered. A tear burned at the side of his eye because in a couple of minutes he wasn't going to be able to breathe.

"They're keeping me on the line." The words were low, but there was a tremor to his voice.

That's when Riley realized his dad still had a phone to his ear and was relaying to someone.

Riley didn't catch what he said next. The crowd around them thickened. Ready to hurl again, Riley took a sip of soda but just spit it in the grass when his tongue wouldn't let him swallow.

Alarm tightened his dad's words as he spoke to the operator. "His eyes are swelling shut and he can't talk…"

Riley tried to blink but dusk was falling in his mind, behind his eyes. Everywhere. Suddenly he heard Saul calling out that he found it.

But something was squeezing Riley's throat shut.

"Someone needs to call 911!" a woman shouted.

"I'm on with them right now!" his dad shouted back.

Then Saul's big, bumbling hands were shoving the EpiPen into Riley's own. Forget the expiration date— Riley hacked at the release with his thumbs, but his fingers weren't working. His throat burned and air didn't come no matter how hard he tried to pull it into his chest.

Then his dad's voice in his ear. "How do we do this?"

A torch was being lit under his lungs. The world that had been spinning suddenly went very still. Which meant he was about to black out. A hot fear slammed his whole body as Riley fought for a breath. He tried to answer but only heard his desperate wheezing. He pointed to the emergency instructions on the label.

His wobbling fingertip just missed the pen entirely.

"Riley!"

His dad grabbed his arm as if to inject the needle. Riley mumbled something about his thigh.

"What?"

Riley patted the top of his leg. "Take the safety off." He coughed again—certain his lungs were tearing in two.

"I can't understand him!" his dad yelled.

That lady from the crowd called out if anyone was a doctor.

Riley needed the EpiPen.

Now.

Still kneeling, he grabbed his dad's hand and fumbled for the safety. His dad flicked it off. Riley felt himself fainting—his head so light, it was about to hit the ground.

He didn't know how he did it, but with his hand still around his dad's, he rammed the needle into his thigh, straight through his jeans. He held it there and it stayed in tight which meant his dad was doing all the work. Riley tried to count to ten but didn't get past four when the world went black.

SEVENTEEN

Stars are amazing things. They tell stories. Map dreams. They're one of the few constants in life…they lead you places. Was it the stars that helped the father get to his boy in the wilderness? Was it the stars that told him which way to go…to hike…to climb? Was it the lights in the sky that led him to his son?

How do you find someone in the middle of nowhere?

Especially when they no longer want to be found.

Head tilted toward the window of the hospital room where he just awoke, Riley stared at the blinking, bright specks in the night.

He didn't know why the audio book was coming to mind as he stared out over the dark cityscape. Maybe he needed to get more sleep. Probably. Because he was pretty sure a star just winked at him. Not cute winked. Creepy winked. Seeing as it was moving, maybe it was just an airplane. The moving, glittering light pulled him back into a trance and he had to blink out of it. What was wrong with him?

Something was messing with his mind because he also had a strange desire to play rugby. And mow the lawn.

Holy smokes, what did they put in his IV?

Riley shifted his arm and looked at the catheter on top of his hand. "Is this really necessary?" he mumbled.

To his surprise, someone answered him. Riley looked over to see a nurse with freckled cheeks and floppy, red hair.

Her smile was tender. "You came to us in pretty bad shape."

He remembered that. With his other hand, Riley rubbed at his eyes. He sat up some and realized that it was nothing but a sheet and a hospital blanket covering him. His clothes were who-knew-where. "How long was I out?"

"A couple of hours. You were awake when you arrived. Do you remember that?"

It was blurry. "Kind of. I remember the ambulance." He was pretty sure there were a few doctors in the mix as well.

"Well, that's good enough for me." She patted his

shoulder with a soft hand.

"What's in this IV?"

"Epinephrine, Benadryl…" she checked the screen on the monitor, "and every ten minutes…zero point five cc's of steroids."

Explained the rugby.

"You may feel jittery or sleepy, but that's normal. I'm watching your heart rate closely."

"I'm really thirsty."

"I'll get you some ice chips."

"Thanks. How's my face?" He didn't mean for that to sound as vain as it was. But he'd been through this before, and chances were, he looked like he'd just been in a fight.

The nurse smiled again when she glanced his way. "Very nice."

Yeah, right. Especially when he reached up and felt the thin tube feeding oxygen into his nose. He blew out a breath, thankful for the sheer sensation of air in his lungs.

The nurse kindly brought him a hand mirror. The swelling around his eyes was a lot better, but he still looked like he'd been put through the wringer. Still, there were some major perks going on. His tongue wasn't swollen anymore, and, thank God, the rash was nearly gone. Come to think of it, he wasn't all that itchy anymore. And he could breathe. This IV was insane.

"Can I get one of these to go?" Riley motioned toward the metal stand and clear bag of liquids.

"Nice try. But I will send you home with prescriptions."

The nurse took his pulse and checked his temperature, then moved to a computer where she typed in the results. Finished, she set the screen to blank and stepped back to the bed. "Take it easy, okay? We're going to monitor you for a few more hours."

Getting cold, Riley ran a hand across his bare chest. "Okay." He shifted his sitting position, feeling a buzz in his veins. He said as much and she adjusted the probe on his finger, then eyed his heart rate on the monitor for several seconds.

"Just try to relax. I'll bring you those ice chips." She fetched him a hospital gown.

He took it, too cold to complain. He'd been through this drill before. "Where's my dad?"

"Just stepped outside to make a couple calls. I'll send him in when he gets back."

"Thanks."

"There's someone else here, too. A man named Saul.

He asks about you every five minutes." She gave him a sweet, sad look. "He's a bit of a wreck."

"Can you send him in?"

"You got it." She stepped out in a flash of purple scrubs and spoke to someone in the hallway before holding the door open for the greatest, hulkiest Mexican Riley had ever known.

Riley couldn't help but grin. "Thanks for running and getting that shot for me, man."

But Saul's eyes were damp and solemn. "I'm so sorry, kid—"

"Hey." Riley pushed himself up more. "It wasn't your fault. I know to watch what I eat and I wasn't paying attention. It was all on me, okay?"

Saul didn't say anything, just sat in the cushioned chair beside the hospital bed.

"*Please* don't feel bad." Riley shifted to put on the hospital gown but just got tangled in the IV cord attached to his hand. Still looking regretful, Saul blinked over at him for a few moments.

"Stop looking at me like I died."

Saul grunted. "You look a whole lot better."

"I *feel* a whole lot better." He tried to untangle himself by unfastening the IV cord but couldn't figure it out. "Did you see my dad?"

"He's outside on the phone with your mom."

"He called her?"

"Yeah. She's about to fly out and save you. He's trying to calm her down." Saul slid a mischievous wink Riley's way, color returning to his face. "He'll tell you all about it."

"Where are we, anyway?" After ringing the nurse for help, Riley moved to the edge of the bed, tugging the blanket along with him.

"About fifteen minutes from the hotel." Saul rose and looked out at the night.

The cold hospital air prickled Riley's skin. He rang again.

"Knock, knock."

Jake stepped in. He shoved hands in his pockets and just looked at Riley for a moment. Finally, he let out a slow breath as if he'd been holding it for a really long time. "Don't scare me like that again, okay?"

"I'll try not to."

"You got your mom freaked out too."

"I can't believe you told her." Riley tried to wrangle the stuck gown into submission.

"Well, I promised I'd tell her if anything exciting

happened…and I'm pretty sure this qualifies."

The nurse came back and fixed Riley's tangled IV by unsnapping the hospital gown along the sleeve. She helped him into it and snapped everything closed.

"What happened to my clothes?" he asked her.

She made a cutting motion with two fingers.

"Really?" That was his favorite band t-shirt. "Jeans?"

"Everything."

Riley glanced to his dad. "You weren't in there… when they…?"

He shook his head, but there was a laugh in his eyes. "But she was." The punk thumbed to the nurse who gave him a caring smile.

"Always the drill with someone in anaphylactic shock to the extent you were," she said.

Riley thought of the rash that had surely flared across his skin. It was mostly gone now, but he still had to fight the urge to scratch his arms. He must have been shivering because she brought out another blanket and draped it over his lap. He asked her about the shot and the expiration date.

She told him that either way it likely saved his life.

Which meant he wouldn't be here if Saul wasn't such a rockstar. Looking to Saul, Riley hoped he'd heard that.

The redheaded woman hung another bag of clear liquid from the IV stand then promised to bring along those ice chips. "I want to get more fluids into you."

Riley adjusted his feet, crossing one over the other. He ran a hand into his hair, wondering what happened to his hat. His wallet and phone were gone too. Then he spotted the things in a big plastic bag on the nearby table. "How long do I have to stay here?" he asked his dad when the nurse was gone.

"Doctor wants to observe you for a couple more hours. It's nine o'clock, so I don't think they're gonna release you 'til morning."

Riley nodded.

His dad gave him a smile that was full of life again. "Cute outfit."

"Very funny." Riley accepted the plastic cup of ice the nurse brought him along with instructions to go slowly. He popped a piece in his mouth and the cold wetness hit the spot. He didn't know he could get that thirsty. "I'm sorry about all this."

His dad moved to perch on the edge of the bed. "Don't be. Hey…" His mouth tipped up. "We have Fox Sports…*and* a bathroom."

Riley smiled. "Win-win."

Stepping forward, Saul squeezed Riley's shoulder. "Glad to see you're okay, *mijo*." Then the huge hand rustled his hair.

Riley gave him a firm handshake. "Thanks."

"I gotta take care of a few calls myself, so I'll leave you two to get some sleep."

Jake gripped Saul's hand and patted him on the back. With a two-fingered wave, Saul stepped out and closed the door.

Riley's dad motioned toward the cushioned chair. "They said I could stay with you, so he'll take the van back to the hotel."

"I don't want you to have to sleep in that chair all night."

Jake moved over to it and sat. "I don't mind. So, say...I scrolled through your contacts and found Becca's mom. I talked to her and let her know what happened, and aside from them being seriously worried about you, I assured them that you're okay. Becca's as freaked out as your mother. I promised we'd see them tomorrow or the next day."

"Are you sure?"

"Yeah. They're lettin' you out of here soon. But I think you'll have to wait for some kind of doctor's clearance—"

"I mean about this trip."

Jake cocked his head to the side. "What do you mean?"

"The Wave of the Winter."

"Oh." He sat back in his chair.

Somewhere down the hall, the elevator dinged. A couple of nurses chatted as they walked by.

Jake looked to the dark window, then back to Riley. "Will you just trust me on that one? Let me make the call? I promise I know what I'm doing."

"Were you headed to the North Shore? When I called you that day I was stuck?"

His dad adjusted his shoes and toed a corner of the faux-tile floor. "Yeah."

A melting piece of ice dripped in Riley's fingers. "And that's what you had to figure out, wasn't it? The tickets you had to cancel and all that."

He nodded.

"Why—"

The door opened. "Riles Kane?"

Riley startled the same second his dad did.

A doctor in a white coat stepped in. Tall and slender, his receding hairline made a spot for the overhead lights to reflect. "I'm Dr. Pratt. And I'm really glad to see you awake. How are you feeling?"

"Feeling all right." Riley ate the melting piece of ice and wiped his fingers.

Wheeling over a small computer stand, the doctor punched in a password and in seconds, Riley's chart lit the screen. Next came the explanation about *sudden circulatory collapse* and *anaphylactic shock,* which was pretty much code for *don't eat shrimp.*

After snapping on gloves, the doctor pressed on Riley's stomach, then checked his skin for the lingering rash. He finished by going over his oxygen levels. "We're going to try and have you out of here tomorrow. We'll take out the oxygen first and if you can stay stable, you'll get your release papers."

Riley nodded.

"You'll be weak for a few days and may experience some nausea. Also, you'll probably find yourself short of breath. I'll be prescribing you an inhaler and," he clicked the mouse, then tapped a few words into his chart, "a new epinephrine shot. Which you'll keep on you at all times?" He looked over at Riley—equal parts stern and kind.

"Yes, sir."

"And we'll get you on your way again." He tapped a

pen on his knee, then slipped it into his coat pocket. "Your dad's told me you're on a road trip." The side of his mouth lifted...as if he wouldn't mind taking one himself.

Riley braved that glance and his dad gave him a sad smile.

After a few last instructions, the doctor shook Riley's hand and promised to be back in a few hours.

Silence fell when he left.

Jake turned the remote on the bedside table. Around and around and around. He tapped it, then ran palms down the sides of his jeans. The track lighting behind him glinted off his slicked, black hair. "I'm sorry if it seems like I lied to you." The chair squeaked when he leaned forward to loosen his silver watch. "In all honesty, I'd still like to do some surfing down in Texas and I might be able to find someone to compete against to make the story totally legit..." His mouth lifted. "It will depend on Saul and what he's up for. But I think I'm gonna try and make sure he heads to Hawaii."

"Is Saul going to be in trouble?"

"Not really. Sponsors understand...and they've got other guys in the lineup, you know? And when I told Saul what was going down...he was packed for the road before

I was, I think."

Riley smiled.

But his dad went serious. "I didn't want to do that to him…but you called and said you needed help, and I just wanted to be there. So I thought fast—and that deal about Texas is what I came up with."

Wanted to be there. Riley tried not to let those words sink in. Words like that had never been meant for him.

But they found their way in anyway.

Which had him asking… "*Why*?"

"Why what?"

"Why do you want to be here? With me? You never wanted it before."

His dad's expression changed—brows tipping up, dark eyes sparkling with what—

Regret?

Was such a thing even possible with Jake Kane? If so…was it enough? Riley remembered his own statement from a few days ago. Of his dad being ten years too late. He swallowed hard. "I *needed* you." The sentiment—the vulnerability—might have embarrassed him, but it didn't. Not here, now, in this moment. Not after he'd waited almost his whole life to say that. So Riley said it again.

His dad lowered his head.

"And you weren't there."

Eyes closed, Jake drew in a slow breath. Then he nodded gently.

"Any chance you want to tell me why that was?"

He looked at Riley as if knowing 'I'm sorry' just wouldn't cut it. He'd be right. "I…just…I just always lived for myself." Leaning forward, he rested his forearms to his knees and smoothed broad palms back and forth. "After my dad died, my mom had a hard time keeping a handle on me. It was like I just stopped caring about anything outside of me. So I poured myself into my sport and a life that made me feel happy. And good." He ran his thumb across his mouth, then held out a hand. "Like I was on top of the world. I had anything I wanted at my fingertips. Money, fame…girls."

A pair of almond-shaped eyes flashed through Riley's mind. So beautiful and so faithful to his dad—and to him—that it made him ache. Because his dad wasn't the only one who didn't deserve her.

They sat quiet for awhile, Riley trying to think of what to say to that. They also had something else in common. Losing someone. Maybe that was a good place to start. "How old were you when your dad died?"

"I was thirteen."

His chest constricted. "I'm really sorry."

Jake swallowed—his face flooded with grief as if he didn't deserve that. "Thanks."

Riley made sure to speak softly. "He died at sea?"

With a tug on his gray shirt, Jake leaned back and propped a foot up on one of his knees. "Yeah. Swept away in a storm."

Riley's mind flooded with images of water and wind and sky. A ship and the vast, open blue. His heart hurt. "What was he like?"

His dad's brows lifted as if not expecting the questions. But they had time, and thanks to this IV, Riley was wired.

"Um…he was kind of stern. He didn't talk a lot. Reserved, I guess you could say. He loved his work. His ship, the sea. We used to build boats together. He loved being out on the water and I joined him whenever I could." His smile was bittersweet. "He was real old school, you know? He followed all the old ways. The things he did, and said. Even the way he wrote his name."

"How was that?" Riley sipped a few drops of melted ice then licked his thumb.

Jake's brow knit tight. "Um…" Looking a bit lost, he glanced around. Patted his pockets. Then his gaze landed on Riley's notebook. Riley handed it over, along with the pen. His dad flipped to the very last page and as he wrote, Riley spoke.

"Did you look like your dad?"

That big smile. "Yeah. We looked *a lot* alike."

Riley smiled as well. For all kinds of reasons. Then he glanced down to see what his dad had written.

Kāne.

Head still bowed, Jake lifted his eyes. "It means *man*."

"Really?"

"I can't remember when I stopped writing it this way." His voice was cool and murky. "Maybe about the time I stopped acting like one."

Riley looked to the paper again—their last name written out as it was meant to be. He mouthed the word— *man*. "That's kind of profound."

His dad seemed amused. "Probably best for us not to get too carried away since it's also splashed across every other bathroom door in Hawaii."

Riley chuckled.

A light hit his dad's eyes. He stood slowly and flicked off the wall switch beside the bed. The room went nearly black, except for the glow from the monitor.

"You need to get some sleep now. Especially since you're gonna have a bunch of calls from two worried ladies in the morning." He stood there, hands in his pockets, looking down on Riley. Stars blinked over his shoulders. After another heartbeat, he bent an arm around Riley's head and gently pulled it against his chest. His thick thumb rubbed against the side of Riley's head. He mumbled into his hair, "Take it easy, okay?"

Eyes closed, Riley swallowed a new kind of burn in his throat. "Okay," he whispered.

EIGHTEEN

They kept him one more day. Riley was about to bust himself out of there when a nurse came in saying that his oxygen saturation was finally better than ninety-two percent. He was off that bed the second they unhooked him.

In the tiny shower of his room, Riley turned on the water full blast until steam rose. He dipped his head under the wet heat and let it pool down his face. Eyes closed, he took shallow, hot breaths and said a prayer of thanks for being alive. And so much more. He stood with water slicking his skin for too long because he got lightheaded. A quick wash of his hair and he got out.

His dad had brought him up a hat and some clothes. Still in the bathroom, Riley tried not to mourn his lost band shirt while he slid a dark gray tee overhead. He had a few other things he was trying not to mourn.

Like Becca's sand dollar…that was no longer whole.

He had the two pieces—the ones Saul had plucked

up from the hotel floor the morning after he'd dumped out Riley's duffle. Determined not to be disappointed, Riley had lain awake last night, holding the broken shell Saul had brought him along with the notepad and pen Riley requested.

The letter was done now. Well, as done as it would ever be. He'd added another two pages while night rolled into morning, then finally stole some sleep. He wished it hadn't taken the trauma of the last two days to show him what his letter was missing, but...sometimes life just works that way.

After jeans, he pulled on his shoes then a hoodie for the cold mountain territory ahead. A final check in the mirror showed that he looked like himself again. Riley tilted his hat a smidge off center, tapped cologne to his skin, and made himself stop thinking about kissing Becca as he reached for the rest of his stuff. According to his dad, they had four hours to go, and with a bag of prescriptions in hand, Riley trailed him out of the hospital room.

His dad walked toward the nurse's station as if not caring who recognized him. And while a few people in the waiting area looked his way, it was Saul who got ambushed.

Nothing like a brave cluster of nurses and a handful of camera phones.

Riley watched near the elevator, and after all the giggling and flashing was over, Saul was still wiping lipstick off his cheek when he joined them. Jake hit the button that closed the door, and as the elevator lowered, Saul discovered the stack of numbers they'd slipped into his back pocket.

Riley and his dad razzed him all the way to the van. Saul opened the back hatch, still grinning, but there was a light in his eyes named Isabel.

Saul rattled the keys. "Who wants to drive?"

"I'll dri—"

"Get in and hush." Jake snatched the keys, the lines around his eyes crinkling.

Riley climbed in the passenger's seat. He shot off a text to his mom that he'd been released, followed by one for Becca that he was on his way. He'd talked to her about a dozen times in the hospital and had caught her up to speed on everything from his blood levels to how much he was looking forward to hanging out with her and her family in the campground.

When his phone buzzed, it was Becca. *I'll be watching for you!*

He smiled. *Did you have a good night?*

Great. I stayed up making you something. You have to pretend to like it, ok?

I promise I'll like it.

She wrote that they were heading out the door but would be back before he arrived. Riley said a quick goodbye before sticking his cell on the charger. The van fell quiet. One block passed and then another.

They were nearly out of town when Riley spoke. "Should we finish our book?" He glanced first to his dad, then to Saul.

Saul thunked his shoulder. "Just waiting for you to hit play, Romeo."

"You're one to talk." Riley adjusted the volume control as the van joined traffic on the 40 again. "So where did we leave off?"

Saul slipped his stack of phone numbers in the door handle. "It was Christmas." He shifted to his other side to free his pack of gum. He popped a piece in his mouth.

"Remember?" Jake added. "The boy's buddy—*Bando*—was there. And his dad finally found him. They were all hanging out in the tree together for a couple of days. Eating turtle soup."

"Oh, yeah. Their little party." Riley hit the play

button. "I think I'm hungry enough to try those acorn pancakes with blackberry jam. I wonder if—"

The narrator began—reading a chapter they'd already heard.

"This is the wrong one. I think we're onto disc number four." Saul held forward the case. "It'll be the last one in there."

Riley flicked the case open. He shuffled through the plastic dividers, but there were only two discs. With the one already in the player, that made three. "Where's the fourth one?"

"It should be there."

Riley held up the evidence. "Not here."

"*What?*"

"There's no disc?" Jake glanced from the case to the road then back to the case. "It's gotta be there somewhere."

"It's not here!" Riley didn't mean for his voice to rise that high. He cleared his throat—aiming for cool. "It's not here," he said again, but was nowhere near to cool because he needed that disc. He needed to know...

Saul muttered in Spanish and dug into his bag.

Riley flipped through the dividers again. "How do you *not* have the whole book?"

"I bought it at a yard sale!"

"And you didn't check?"

"It was a dollar!"

Half panicked, half laughing, Riley ran his hands into his hair. "Okay…we need to calm down and think rationally."

"Yes. Rationally." His dad rubbed at his jaw, not looking rational at all. "Dude. I'm totally depressed about this."

Riley smirked, then remembered what he had in his wallet. Tipping onto his hip, he yanked out the leather folds. He ran his fingers along his cards and whipped out the one the Fletchers had given him for Christmas.

"Score!" He held up the plastic gift card and waggled it. "I got it covered, guys. Stand by…" Chin to chest, he held his phone and searched the download store for the audio book department. He punched in *My Side of the Mountain* and waited for it to appear. Remembering the adaptor cord in his backpack, he pulled it out and hooked his cell up to the van's speakers.

"Is it there?" his dad asked.

"Hold…on." With quick fingers, Riley tapped in the gift card code, and within seconds, the whole book was downloading to his phone. "We got it, *baby*!"

His dad rattled the steering wheel and Saul let out a whoop.

"It's almost done loading."

"Hit play!" Saul smacked his arm.

"I'm trying!" Riley's thumb hovered over the timer icon as it completed the rotation. A checkmark appeared. He tapped the screen.

The story loaded and his heart ticked off the seconds. The narrator's clear voice flooded the vehicle.

The kid was back.

Orange-red bluffs loomed in the distance; not a tree in sight. Telephone poles, a few oil drills. And now...wide-open road. Saul shot a whistle then slid open his window.

Riley pushed his own open and let the wind hit his face. The boy in the wilderness had his falcon. He had his tree house and his friend. But best of all...he had the dad that had scaled a mountain to find him. Maybe he wouldn't stay...but there was the climb...

And it was enough. It had to be enough.

The highway stretched endless and straight in front of them, dry brush and winter desert out every window.

Riley stared past the cracked asphalt of the road. Tumbleweeds were now replaced by trees once again and he wondered when they would hit the very stretch of highway where Becca's dad had crashed. He could barely imagine such a thing. He wished that Jay Fletcher—and his family—didn't have to.

Saul sneezed into his shoulder. Jake drummed a thumb against the door frame. And there was just the whir of tires over asphalt as the van neared the snow-capped mountains. The book had just finished, but no one had broken the silence yet. The story ended well. The kid's whole family came to live in the woods with him. Riley was pretty sure the dad was going to build a cabin for everyone.

His dad and Saul exchanged a look.

Shifting his legs against his backpack, Riley worked at the bent nails.

The van chugged along. Cars loaded down by snowboards and skis passed going the speed limit, if not over. Everyone headed up to the mountain resort town and the slopes. His dad mentioned wishing he had a snowboard. Riley nodded absently. He twisted the bent nails one way and then another. Exactly as he'd been doing for miles upon miles…

Jake spoke. "Just pull them apart."

Riley glanced over.

"Just pull both nails apart… straight out. Nice and slow."

"How do you know?"

"Because they were in your backpack when Saul brought it to the hospital. I figured it out while waiting for you to come to." He gave Riley a look that meant it hadn't been for entertainment.

Riley set his mouth, unsure what to make of any of it. A few seconds later, he had the nails apart. He stared at the two separate pieces in his hand.

"Now what?" his dad asked.

Riley tipped his head to the side. "I can stick the pieces with the sand dollar. They can keep each other company."

Saul snorted. It was followed by another apology.

Riley leaned around his own seat to glance back. "I'm just kidding." He winked.

"Can I have one of those?" his dad asked.

Shrugging, Riley handed one over. His dad nudged the single, bent nail onto the dash. Riley slipped the other in the pouch of his backpack.

The sun hung just over the treetops. The mountain

temperature cool. The campground was lower than the resort town itself, so Riley doubted they'd hit snow. He thought of the generator and how it would enable the Fletchers to be closer to Jay in the hospital.

Riley pressed the passenger window farther open so that the chilly afternoon air gushed in. He adjusted his cap, turning it backwards to keep the bill from lifting up. Riley closed his eyes. What was that phrase again? Unable to think of it, he looked over at his dad. "A perfect wind. How did you say it?"

He smiled. "*Ka makani `olu `olu.*"

Riley peered out his window to the high desert landscape passing by. Dark clouds rolled in from the east, and far away in the blue-gray sky, it looked like it was raining. He breathed deeply and caught the scent. "I wonder if this is one."

His dad slid open his own window and was quiet a moment. "It's definitely one."

The GPS cut in announcing, "*Two miles to destination.*"

Heart suddenly in his throat, Riley shifted his feet. He thought of Becca. What he had to give her. What he didn't.

Riley adjusted his hat. Fiddled with the open

window.

"Nervous?" Jake asked.

"Why would I be nervous?"

"No reason." But his dad smiled.

Riley smiled too because he knew what his dad was getting at. "Maybe a little."

The GPS announced that they were one mile from the campground. Leaning as close to the open window as he could, Riley peered up the highway to towering pines. An upcoming sign showed the symbols of a travel trailer and tent. His heart hit his ribs. The van thunked through a dip, and Saul, who had passed out, grumbled to life. Riley bounced one leg. Then a hand. Finally, his dad told him to take a deep breath and he tried.

When that didn't work, he opened his paper bag and took a shot from his inhaler.

Another chuckle from the man in the driver's seat.

They pulled up to the squat ranger's hut and paid the day use fee. With instructions to find the Fletchers at site 113, Riley sat tight while his dad turned the wheel that direction. Down a narrow, one-way road that was lined with tents and trailers.

105

107

Riley chewed his lip. 109.

That's when he spotted a girl up the way. He unbuckled his seatbelt. She was stooping to pick up a football. Brassy earrings danced against her neck, and he knew those hands. That girly throw. Before Riley could stop himself, he rammed his door open.

NINETEEN

The van barely slammed to a halt before he climbed out.

Riley gave himself two full seconds to take in the sight of her—brown hair pulled up in a messy bun. Leggings under a long sweater. And that smile...the one that had sun and life in it.

He called her name.

She looked his way and her eyes went wide. Before he knew it, she was running toward him. Arms around his neck, Becca Fletcher collided into him so hard he hit the van. His hat fell off.

She smelled like flowery lotion and every good thing he could think of.

"You're here." Burying her face in his neck, that sound filtered through her voice—the one that meant she was trying not to cry.

He squeezed tighter, one arm around her waist, the other sliding up to hold the back of her head. "It's a miracle."

She laughed, then sniffed. She was so warm…and soft…and perfect.

Riley closed his eyes, having never known that simply holding someone could feel so good. Though he wanted to hold on longer, they had an audience. And not just the two surfers in the van. A whole family on bikes was riding by and some little girls giggled as they ran past chasing a Frisbee.

Riley released her. But Becca smoothed the back of her fingers over his cheek, then into his hair. She peered up as if seeing him for the first time. For him, he was pretty sure he'd seen her a million times in his mind—in a million little ways. Like pieces of her—who she was—lit him up from the inside. He realized that she was looking at him not as if for the first time. She was looking at him the same. In that million-pieces kind of way.

Riley gripped the side of her neck, ran his thumb against her jaw, then made himself speak before he forgot himself again. "You can meet my dad."

Nodding, Becca glanced to the van. The guys climbed out then as if that was their cue. Jake gave Becca a hug. Saul kissed her hand.

Becca beamed.

Maybe he was mistaken, but Riley was pretty sure

his dad did as well.

Riley glanced from the trailer with its open door, to the chairs circled around the fire pit, to the dirt path that meandered toward the next site. "Where is everybody?"

"Oh, Mom took them on a walk for the afternoon." She looped one hand through his and motioned with the other toward a rise in the trees. "There's an alpine vista that's about an hour hike away. I was going to go, but then when we heard you were close, I stayed back just in case." She squeezed his hand, then the other joined it.

Riley liked that.

"They've been gone awhile, so they'll be back soon."

"Saul's in need of the little boy's room," Jake blurted. "So he and I are going to walk up to the nearest bathroom. We'll be back in a few." He started off, and with a wink, Saul did too.

Riley owed them one.

A few seconds later, it was just him and Becca.

"I'm in awe," she said, still holding his hand with both of hers. "You're here. And even your dad." She leaned her forehead into his shoulder and he breathed deep. "And you're alive." Her grip squeezed tighter. "Don't do that again."

He kissed the top of her head and it was the most

natural thing in the world. "I'll do everything I can not to," he said softly. "If it's any comfort, I promised about five different people—" including her—"that I will keep that shot with me all the time."

The next thing he knew, she was leading him to the trailer, asking how he was feeling and if he needed to sit down.

Riley chuckled. "I'm just fine."

Up the trailer and inside…

He stopped in the doorway, but she was on some kind of mission as she disappeared into the back bedroom, returning not a moment later. Canvas tote in hand, she looked at him with a trace of shyness.

Becca rattled the bracelets on her wrist. "Don't worry…you can laugh." Bending, she pulled something out and unfolded a portion of cloth.

That's right. She'd made him something. The shirt designs she'd been working on?

No. Riley's brow lifted. Aside from the skateboard print on the fabric, he recognized it as something he used to have. A holder for his EpiPen. He could see now why she was worried he'd laugh. But there was nothing funny about what she held. The fact that she'd sewed it…and he knew they didn't have a machine…

"Mom drove me into town to the fabric shop. I couldn't sleep at all when you were in the hospital, so I worked on this..." She unfolded the holder all the way, then peeked up at him. "What do you think?"

"It's totally cool."

She rolled her eyes—downplaying his words—and her cheeks went a shade more pink. "Should we see if it fits?"

"Yeah."

Thinking to take the holder from her, he eased up his shirt...just as she started to reach around him. They both froze.

"Oh, sorry." He lowered his shirt.

"No, it's fine. That's how it will be worn." She fumbled the holder, dropping it.

They nearly clunked heads when they both bent for it.

He spared her any further awkwardness by taking the thing from her. Raising his shirt again, he slipped the strip of fabric around his stomach, and his fingers and brain took a few seconds to figure out the clasp she'd made. Finished, he looked at her. With hours of worry and what felt a heck of a lot like love wrapped around his waist, he asked her if it looked right.

"Perfect." A brightness lit her eyes. "It's just…inside out."

It was?

He looked down, his hair falling into his eyes. He brushed it away just as her arms slipped around him, the tips of her fingers sliding along his back as she tucked the holder in the other way.

Riley wet his lips.

He held still, trying really hard to focus on the shape of her earrings instead of the way her soft fingers smoothed the fabric against his side. He swallowed hard. There wasn't a whole lot between them except the silence and the way his cologne mixed with her lotion. Riley slid his gaze to her heart-shaped face, wondering what she was thinking.

From the furrow of her brow, he looked to the thin chain draping her neck…near the patch of shoulder peeking out of her oversized sweater.

He cleared his throat and she twisted the rest of the fabric at his stomach. She sure was taking her sweet time. Her eyes were wide and wondering when she glanced at his face and slowly pulled away.

"I need to remember to put it on backwards every time," he blurted.

She smiled.

Riley lowered his shirt.

Becca nudged the hem up to adjust one final spot before letting it fall again. "If you don't want to wear it this way, you can also hook the clip to a keychain or attach it to your backpack, or even your belt."

"Really?"

"I tried to draw it up to work different ways, but..." She scrunched her nose. "It's kind of hokey, isn't it?"

Reaching under his tee, Riley unclasped it just so he could see it better. Her stitches were tiny and even. Homemade—all heart. His little Gypsy. He looked at her. "It's the best thing anyone's ever made me." He took her hand and kissed her palm, then spoke to clear his head. "I have something for you, too." Riley glanced over his shoulder to the van. "I'll go grab it."

She folded the strip of fabric and set it aside. "I'll come with you."

Taking her hand again, he led her out and around to the passenger side of the van, wishing he didn't have to let go to get the clunky door open. On the floor was his backpack and he unzipped the front pouch.

"Here..." he said quietly as he turned back to her.

Becca's eyes danced over what he held. "Half a sand

dollar?"

"Yeah. It was actually whole when I found it…but it kind of cracked when Saul dumped out my bag to find my shot."

Her brows shot up.

"Would it be okay if I still gave it to you? Or what's left of it?" He ducked his head, not really knowing how to put to words what he was thinking. But he made himself find them. Find the words to say that it wasn't the first time something perfect had to be broken so he could be saved. Humbled by the life and grace that had been given to him, Riley took what he had and slipped it into her hand. He also gave her the letter. It was super thick and sloppy-looking without an envelope, but her eyes went glassy then wet.

"I finished it in the hospital and was on a lot of meds, so if I said anything stupid, just ignore it. Also, I'm sorry about my handwriting."

She swiped at a tear and clutched the pages to her sweater as she peered up at him.

"And Becca?" He swallowed hard. Because this next bit was something he hadn't wanted to put in her letter. There were just some things that needed to be said out loud. He owed her nothing less. "There are a couple of girls out there that deserve an apology. A few sets of parents too." Slowly, he shook his head and made himself look at her. "I'm sorry that you have to be around for this—and that I didn't do it sooner—but if you'll bear with me through it…I think it's something I need to do."

She nodded gently and her voice was soft. "Whatever you need. I'll be there."

When her eyes grew wetter, he knew she was giving more than he deserved. How he hated this. The fact that he wasn't innocent. Wasn't whole in the way she was.

But she closed her fingers around the broken shell and said that she was going to keep it safe. That she was going to keep it forever.

And he learned in that moment just how much love could make you ache.

Riley stepped closer, cupped the side of her face. He ran his thumb against the chain that draped the dip of her neck, thinking of doing the same to her mouth. But something inside him told him not to.

Maybe it was the fact that his dad and Saul were now in lawn chairs a few yards away. Maybe it was the fact that he'd yet to meet her own father. Introduce himself. Do this right. Perhaps it had to do with the fact that— unlike with girls in the past—he knew he needed to keep his hands to himself.

Or maybe it had something to do with the fact that CJ was walking past chanting, "Riley and Becca sittin' in a tree. K-I-S-S-I-N-G."

Probably a little bit of everything.

Anna skipped up giggling, and Mrs. Fletcher released the double stroller handle long enough to wave. Her hiking boots were covered in dust and her jeans had little muddy hand prints on one side. Jake and Saul rose and strolled that way in greeting.

CJ was still singing. "First comes...comes..." His voice went faint as he asked his older sister what came first.

Becca blushed three shades of pink. Riley took her hand, kissed her fingers instead.

She kissed his cheek. "*That smile*...and a dimple to go with it."

Looking down, Riley chuckled. "I don't have dimples." But he did when he smiled. Suddenly self-conscious, he pursed his lips to fight it, but that only ever made it worse. "Hey...how about that generator?"

Her eyes laughed and poor CJ was still mumbling to himself, trying to figure out the words to that chant. Riley looked over to see his dad talking to Mrs. Fletcher. Jake shook her hand and Riley thumbed toward the van.

He opened the back hatch and lifted out his duffle, setting it aside. Tyler and Anna gathered around and CJ hoisted one of the twins out of the way. Becca plucked up the other boy and propped the three-year-old on her hip. After pulling out the water jugs, Riley carried them into the campsite. His dad and Saul hefted out the generator. Mrs. Fletcher thanked them all a hundred times.

Once the beast was in place, Riley got to work. It took a couple minutes to hook the generator up, and he finished by filling the small tank with gas. He primed the tank, then flipped the switch. A couple seconds later, the power source gurgled and sputtered. But nothing.

He primed the tank again, then pressed the red switch. The generator gurgled again. Sputtered. Riley made a few adjustments. Flicked the switch a third time. It groaned to life a few seconds later.

Mrs. Fletcher hurried inside and within seconds came back out. "Heats on! It works!"

The kids shouted and Becca did a dance with little Anna.

"We can go closer to the hospital," Mrs. Fletcher said in a teary voice.

Tyler just jumped up and down. The twins clapped

their hands, probably having no idea what was going on.

"I can't thank you enough." Mrs. Fletcher all but glowed as she looked between Riley, his dad, and Saul. "I've been promising these kids sloppy joes as soon as we got back. You guys hungry?"

Starving, come to think of it.

Saul followed Mrs. Fletcher into the trailer and Riley heard him asking how he could help.

Mrs. Fletcher's sloppy joes were really good. So was the dip Saul made. And the company? Couldn't have been better. But the meal passed too quickly. Much too quickly. Because the next thing Riley knew, CJ was carrying a package of marshmallows over to the fire ring—the sun was nearly gone—and Jake was standing by the van, keys in hand.

The whole world slowed.

The Hawaiian had his hands crammed in his pockets and watched the orange sky with a focused expression. Jaw hard...gaze far away.

This was it, then. The end of the road.

Not knowing what to say, Riley walked over and checked the back of the van for any more of his stuff. He'd bought a tent a couple hundred miles back and hauled it out. There was nothing else. Saul walked over, joining Jake in quiet conversation.

Riley looked to the two of them. "You guys have to take off, don't you?"

His dad set his mouth and pulled a sweater out through the open van window. "Saul here has some stuff he needs to take care of." He looked over at Riley, but the regret lasted only a second until he pulled the sweater on overhead. He spent a moment straightening the hood. "In this place called Hawaii."

Riley looked to Saul. "You're going after all?" Something good washed through him. It felt a lot like surprise. A lot like happiness. But the bittersweet kind.

Saul ruffled an oversized hand through sun bleached hair. "I need to be there. Made some commitments to a couple folks that I don't think I can cancel." He turned the ring on his thick pinkie, then shot out an elbow to the man beside him. "Someone's gotta be there to show those rookies how it's done and I've been trying to see if I can drag this yahoo along with me."

Riley swallowed a burn in his throat. "Go, Dad."

Slowly, Jake shook his head. "I dunno—"

"Please." Riley nudged his dad's shoulder. The last of the sun vanished. Cool shadows took its place. "You have to. Please."

Jake gently thumped the side of his fist against the van as if the notion didn't mean a thing to him.

"Saul, get this guy on a plane." The words slipped out because they needed to be said. "You two need to be there." Riley swallowed the growing lump in his throat.

The one that told him he would miss it all.

The two guys exchanged glances. After glimpsing his watch, Saul hitched open the driver's side door. He slipped his wallet out of his pocket and onto the dash. He gave Riley one of his bear hugs along with a whispered *mijo*. My boy.

Riley slammed his eyes closed when they stung. He gripped Saul's shoulder, unsure of what to do. It was the first time a man had ever hugged him.

Saul climbed in the driver's seat and Riley stood beside his dad. He crammed his hands in his pockets, not quite looking at the man beside him. "It was good seeing you."

His dad nodded.

"Thanks...thanks for the ride." Riley glanced over. "And for everything."

His dad's eyes were glassy. "It was my pleasure." He gripped Riley in a hug with a tightness that rivaled Saul's. In fact, it was tighter. "You take care of that girl of yours."

Riley promised that he would. He thought of his mom then as well. He wondered if his dad might have too.

Saul opened the driver's side window and leaned an elbow out, watching.

"I'll see ya soon, 'K?" Jake whispered.

Riley nodded and pulled away, trying to clear his throat against the tightness. "See you soon. Have fun."

His dad nodded. "We will." Gripping the passenger side door, he gave one last nod to Riley, then waved toward the Fletchers. Rising from her chair, Becca waved in return.

Swinging his gaze back to the Volkswagen, Riley watched his dad climb in and slam the door. The motor chugged to life, sending the boards on top to vibrating. The skateboard his dad had given him was no longer strapped snug beside them. Saul reached up and adjusted the rearview mirror. He waved and Riley rubbed fingers against the base of his hurting throat.

The van pulled forward, easing into a U—heading back the way it had come. Riley stepped back. His dad put an arm out the passenger window, lifting a hand. Riley lifted one back...then crammed his hands in his pockets and watched the Volkswagen drive away.

It came then. He meant to fight it…but it came.

The whole world went damp. *It's enough. You don't ask for more.* It was enough. Riley smeared the back of his hand over his eyes, then stood there and watched the best week of his life drive out of sight.

It was enough. And he wasn't eight anymore.

Something buzzed in his back pocket. He worked the phone out only to see that it was a text from his dad.

I wish you were coming with us.

Riley smiled and swiped the heel of his palm over one eye, then the other. *Next time.*

His dad wrote back that it was a deal.

The sun dipped and was gone. The air dropped a few degrees then and there. Chilled, but not quite ready to join that fire *just* yet, Riley's thumb hovered over the keypad. The words Becca had sent him came to mind, so he tapped them out.

Aloha wau ia 'oe.

He hit send and shot out a breath—having realized how long he'd wished for a dad to say that to. His cell buzzed a few seconds later and he smiled when words flashed across the screen. All in caps. The very same ones.

TWENTY

April 5

"So I add these tangerine sections to the salad?" Becca asked.

Chef's knife in hand, Saul peeked over her shoulder. "Yup. Just toss them in, *mija*." He added fresh cilantro, then sprinkled in slices of cherry tomatoes.

Becca's bracelets clanked together as she plucked up the wooden salad spoons and mixed it all together. Riley watched from the barstool—still amazed that two whole people could fit in his tiny excuse for a kitchen.

"Hey, Useless." Saul waved his knife toward Riley. "Fetch me the vinaigrette."

In the fridge, Riley found a bowl of salad dressing along with a whiff of lime. "This looks amazing."

"*Gracias*." Saul worked his knife against a cutting board, dicing the chicken he'd spent half the morning roasting.

Riley handed the dressing to Becca, then kissed her on the cheek.

That very cheek appled in a smile as she poured in the vinaigrette. "All right, Useless. Out you go…" Becca nudged him in the stomach and Riley decided to make himself useful.

He put plates in a stack on the counter and nabbed a handful of mismatched forks. Plastic cups. Napkins printed with race car flags. Not exactly the greatest Easter setup, but it's what he had. There wasn't a place for everyone to sit at a table, so Riley hoped people wouldn't mind holding plates in their laps.

The day before, Becca had strung Christmas lights around the windows which made his cabin feel cooler than it actually was. Plugging them in, Riley glimpsed the magazine photo tacked to the wall. The one he'd torn out of Sports Illustrated a few weeks ago.

There, in the centerfold, was a laughing Saul. Dressed in jeans and a tank, he was being doused by a bottle of foamy champagne from his greatest competitor, Jake Kane. The Hawaiian surfer had an arm around his best friend's bulky, brown shoulders as Saul balanced a huge cardboard check with his own name on it. Made out for twenty-five thousand dollars.

Touching a corner of the magazine photo, Riley reread the part about how Saul had donated every penny to breast cancer research in honor of Isabel. Riley glanced over at Saul who sang along to the radio. Some heroes didn't wear capes. Some drove semis while others wore Kiss the Chef aprons. At least the best ones did, anyway.

Riley nearly jumped when a snowball smacked the window. It slid down the glass in a melting mess. Grabbing his jacket, he slipped an arm through the first sleeve as he stepped onto the porch. Leaning on the railing gave him a safe spot to survey the mayhem. His dad was in the yard, outnumbered five to one as little Fletchers used him for target practice. The guy was soaked in snow.

While Easter was always cold here, it was the first time in a few years that a storm like this had come through. Jake ducked when a slushy snowball sailed past his head. The surfer slipped, fell, and the twins tackled him. A few yards away, Jay Fletcher laughed from his chair. Another chair cradled his cast that would come off soon. Grinning beside him, Mrs. Fletcher sipped from a cup of cider. Flames crackled in the fire pit in front of them.

"I think I need to get a video of this," Riley called out to his dad. "Put it on YouTube."

Bending, Jake formed a quick snowball and pelted it at one of the kids. "You watch it." With a laugh, he ducked, but a snowball smacked him in the side of the head and he fell again.

Riley chuckled and used the slush on the railing to make a good-sized ball. When his dad tried to get up, he hurled it that way and pelted him square in the back. Which was dumb. Because five minutes later, he was on the ground in the snow with two little Fletchers on his stomach while his dad rubbed snow in his hair. It was up his shirt and down his pants and he was doing that horrible screech thing that no guy his age should ever do.

"Holler enough!" CJ chanted.

Riley knocked him over and gave a laughing CJ a taste of his own medicine.

From their chairs beside the fire pit, Becca's mom said the kid deserved it. Jay took a picture with an old camera. A smile lifted his bushy, red beard.

CJ wriggled free and Riley lunged after him, trying not to topple Anna in the process. Riley gave her a high five when CJ hollered, "Enough!"

Jake was brushing snow from his hair as he walked

over to where Jay sat. Riley's dad held his hands out to the flames and spoke to Jay who tapped his propped-up cast as he answered. After a sip from her mug, Mrs. Fletcher laughed at whatever they had said. Riley went to join them, but then Saul called out that dinner was ready.

"But my mom's not here yet." Realizing how soaked he was, Riley started toward the house for dry clothes.

His dad stepped up beside him, their shoulders brushing as they walked across the yard. "She hit traffic on the 101."

Riley glanced over. "How do you know that?"

"'Cause I spoke to her a little while ago."

Eyebrows lifting, Riley looked at his dad.

"What?"

Riley smirked as he held the door open.

"She answers my calls *sometimes*."

Becca and her parents filed in, Jay like a pro on his crutches. Then it was a few minutes of peeling off jackets and hats and finding places to stash it all. Jake added a log to the fire in the little wood-burning stove. Deciding to clear out some of the coats so people could sit, Riley snagged an armful and started for his room.

In the back bedroom, he dropped a few on the black and gray plaid comforter. The really wet ones he hung on the end of his propped-up snowboard. Riley changed quickly and dug for a too-small shirt that might fit CJ. At the sound of a horn cheerfully honking, he opened his bedroom door and nearly smacked into Becca.

"They just spotted your mom's car so she'll be here in a sec." Becca held a few more jackets out to him, then winked. "Your dad's *pacing*."

Riley couldn't fight the smile. Poor guy.

He held up the smallish tee. "Will this fit CJ?"

"Yeah." She took it, then looked at the dry one he'd just put on. Her pretty eyebrows danced. "Nice shirt."

Riley rubbed a hand over his chest. "I'm kind of fond of this one."

Becca scrunched her nose playfully.

For Valentine's, he'd asked her what she wanted to do and she'd asked to go to a concert. A musician they had recently discovered and loved was playing in Los Angeles. Riley jumped at the chance to do one of his favorite things in the world, and to honor her parents' wishes, he set it up for them to go with another couple— Ramsey and the girl he was seeing. She and Becca were pals before Riley's buddy could even park.

The four of them had waited in line beneath the theatre's sign lit up with *Josh Garrels,* and the concert was easily one of Riley's favorites. To make it better, the musician's discussions were amazing. The profound things he shared shone through in the way that he lived his life and wrote his songs. Like he was the son of a Good King and treated people as if they could be too. Riley kind of wished his dad had been there. So he went over to the merch table and got a couple of CDs. And a new t-shirt.

Dressed in jeans and a blouse, Becca had waited on a nearby stool. She was pretty as a picture with a potted palm dripping twinkle lights beside her. Apparently some guy thought so too, because Riley overheard her answer to whatever was said.

"I'm sorry... I have a boyfriend."

And that was him, on cloud nine, walking back to her.

On the way home, he had put his arm across the backseat where they were sitting and she'd nestled in against him, her head to his shoulder as they often sat. He'd looked out at the night—took in the sights of the LA skyline moving past as they headed out of the city.

"When You Gonna Run" by Alpha Rev had been playing soft through the speakers and Riley had been playing with the ends of Becca's hair. It was totally dark and she was terribly near, but there was something about not being alone that made him trust he could keep his head above water. He'd barely had to move to kiss her, and the next thing he knew, he was passing from old to new. It was probably only five seconds of his life, and while he was already ruined for any other girl in this world, the sweetness and warmth of Becca put the G in *goner*.

She was a gift to him, and for some reason, she treated him the same. It was a kind of love that he was still trying to make sense of, but he aimed to keep at it. He had to.

Riley followed Becca into his living room just as his dad headed out the front door. People were everywhere. Now he knew the meaning of the term *bursting at the seams*. But it was a good kind of bursting, and when he glimpsed the silver sedan pulling into his driveway, he knew it was about to get even better.

Through the open front door Riley glimpsed his dad jogging out to her car. The backseat was loaded with boxes which had to be the shirts for the surf camp. Well, surf *and* skate camp, since Riley had promised to come out of hiding. His dad had reminded him that pro boarder or not, life would always be what he made it. What Riley wanted was to do everything he could for the Fletchers. On top of it all, his dad's biggest sponsor had stepped in and donated a bunch of gear for the camp. That was pretty cool in Riley's book.

Thanks to his mom stepping in to organize the fundraiser, registration was full and the waiting list so long, they were already discussing a second camp. Saul and Mrs. Fletcher had all the meals planned out and Becca was primed to go as one of the girl counselors.

His mom was going to be the other.

That very woman had a sack of drinks in her hand which Jake hurried to take for her. He said something that Riley couldn't hear, but what he did catch was the lift to his mom's mouth. She was trying to fight it. Riley could tell in the way she looked away, but whatever Jake had said must have been something else, because she full on smiled at the man as she rose from the driver's seat.

And Riley thought back to the line his dad had finally added to his autographed postcard last night after arriving. *Mahalo e ke akua no keia la.* Riley smiled. Saul had been conked out on the couch and there Riley and his dad sat. Coffee cups, bent nails, and feather-soft pages of mercy on the table between them.

Giving Riley a chance to recall the final words he'd

written in Becca's letter...

That there are some things you can't go back from. You just lay the broken pieces down and then there's grace and its glue, and in a strange way, you're more whole than before, because this time...

This time it's not by your own doing.

Now Riley looked out the window as his dad took the second sack his mom had to offer. Side by side, the two started toward the house. Not very quickly. Even though his mom took a demure step away, gaze on the path in front of her, she was seriously making a day of a thirty-foot walk. His dad wasn't watching where he was going at all.

Becca stepped up beside Riley and laced her small fingers into his.

"Look at my dad." Riley kissed the top of her head. "Guy's got stars in his eyes."

And he knew. That whether or not it was the stars that led the dad up that mountain, it was a choice to seek. A choice to stay. And come what may...

Come what may...

There was *mahalo e ke akua no keia la*. Thanks be to God for this day.

NOTE TO READERS

Thank you for letting me write stories that might make you wonder. It's an honor each time a reader spends quiet hours among words that I had the privilege of penning and when those moments of curiosity arise, I imagine you wondering—and in a way *creating*—right alongside me. May I rest my chin in my hand and ask you, "What do you think is going to happen next?" I'll smile as you answer, because my friend, you're onto something.

It's the reason that I write. To fill in the gaps of the unknowns that draw the imagination. To take questions about life and faith and pour them out onto the page so that I can see a glimpse of what might be. I have no doubt that you read to do the same. Like Riley, Jake, and Saul as they eagerly await the final lines to their audio book, here's to sweet endings.

Keep wondering, friends, and I will do the same. If those

musings have you curious about these characters, know that I'm always an email away. Your notes have made me laugh, they've made me cry happy tears, and they never cease to fill my heart. If those wonderings are about the God who gives the kind of grace that's glue, I hope you'll visit www.joannebischof.com/wildairhope, or drop me a note. Together we can pour imaginary cups of coffee, and talk about bent nails and feather soft pages of mercy.

Until we meet again – God speed on your own adventures. May you *"live in the sunshine, swim the sea"* and *"drink the wild air."*

Mahalo, friends.

BEHIND THE SCENES

To Get to You began as a short story called "The Balsam Walk." Written from Becca's eyes and heart when she first meets Riley, it's published in a short story anthology, *21 Days of Christmas*. It was an absolute delight to write and after finishing that little 1,700 word tale, I wanted to know what might happen next. Within moments *To Get to You* was born, and this historical author took her first big step into the world of contemporary fiction.

Set in my home town in Southern California, the idea seemed easy enough. But what began as an unfolding of the rest of Becca and Riley's love story sent me on an adventure I never expected. Becca threw everyone quite a surprise! Next thing I knew, it was suddenly the inside of a 1965 VW Samba, the desert air—cool and dry—and a couple of professional surfers along for the ride.

Reminding me once again that God has a greater purpose than we can see. Here's to the twists in story…and life.

Jake Kane's career was inspired by that of pro surfer, Kelly Slater, who with eleven ASP World Tour wins, and a love for the waves, is iconic to the sport. Not only did he spearhead the documentary for the Wave of the Winter on Hawaii's North Shore, but he also won the contest when he was the same age as Jake…and Saul.

If you are ever as far west as one can get in the USA, I hope you'll have the chance to drive along the Pacific Coast Highway, one of my favorite ways to see the ocean. The slow going? Completely worth it—especially around sunset. Our favorite vehicle to take is my husband's black Jeep. Of course, he would want you to know that it runs much better than Riley's. Be sure to grab an In-N-Out burger along the way. You'll thank me later.

Oh…and that feed store and Christmas tree lot? It's on the farm where my husband grew up. He sold more bags of feed than he could ever count and not only mastered the art of "tree installation", but proposed to me there one Christmas eve…shortly after piling the left over trees on the side of the road.

ACKNOWLEDGMENTS

The greatest thanks to God for working a million little miracles along the journey of this book. For putting just the right friends into my path, and for being the strength behind this story when I felt so very small. This story would not have been possible if it weren't for the wonderful heart and talent of my dear friend, Amanda Dykes, who stepped in to give this story a top-notch critique and cheered me on each step of the way.

Thank you to local friends: my teen beta-readers Kara Swanson and Kezia Manchester for reading the manuscript then responding with lots of exclamation points. You two are awesome! And to Cathie Davis (the greatest neighbor and nurse I know) for letting me sit in your kitchen and ask gobs of questions on anaphylactic shock and Riley's hospital stay. I made Riley's nurse red-headed because I can't think of anyone who would have taken better care of him than you.

A special, special thanks to calligrapher, Mindy Sato, for embracing this story from the start and for creating the arrow nestled in these pages…and so much more. I'm honored to call you my friend.

A heart-full-of-gratitude to Sally Bradley and Denise Harmer not only for your excellent editing of this manuscript but for your sweet encouragement along the way. Also, a big thanks to Andrea Cox for once again proofing my work and helping to make it shine.

To Brittany McEuen for inspiring me to be brave enough to put the first two chapters of this book online when I was terrified and to my beautiful family: Mom, Dad and Kiddos. You are the lights of my life. And lastly, to my husband, Noah, for making sure that Riley never threw a manual transmission into park, that the engine was at the right end of the VW, and for reading this manuscript from cover to cover like a champ. You are the coolest half of Mason Jar Books and my hero.

Two-time Christy Award-finalist and author of *This Quiet Sky* and the Cadence of Grace series, **Joanne Bischof** has a deep passion for stories that shine light on God's grace and goodness. She lives in the mountains of Southern California with her husband and their three children. You can visit her website at www.joannebischof.com or find her on Instagram - @masonjarbooks.

JOANNE BISCHOF

Meet Ramsey & Sienna in

A Boy and Wild Horses

Wild
Air
n o v e l

BOOK TWO

#wildairseries

MORE FROM JOANNE

THIS QUIET SKY

Carol Awards Finalist

Christy Awards Finalist

Grace Awards Finalist

Readers' Favorite 5-star seal

Made in the USA
Middletown, DE
17 June 2019